STING OF THE HONEYBEE

Also by Frank Parrish

FIRE IN THE BARLEY

STING
OF THE HONEYBEE

A Novel of Suspense

Frank Parrish

DODD, MEAD & COMPANY • NEW YORK

STING OF THE HONEYBEE

'Readeeeee – steadeeeee – go!' called Dan Mallett.

Two of the children kicked their ponies into a canter. They started off on the bending race, weaving between the white sticks that Dan had earlier stuck into the grass of the paddock. A third child screamed at her pony, and persuaded it at last into a bouncing trot. The fourth, a very small boy with a scarlet face, was carted sharply backwards towards a tiny crowd of spectators, who wailed and scattered.

Dan ran to the pony and grabbed the bridle. He heaved it forward in the right direction. The pony accepted this, having known Dan all its life, and joined without enthusiasm in the race.

'That's cheatin',' said the purple mother of one of the other contestants.

'We'll worry about that if he wins,' said Dan. He spoke mildly, so as not to enrage the mother (it always surprised him how enraged they became when their children were involved in any competition). But he used his bank-manager voice, which was one of his many voices, so the woman wouldn't think she could browbeat him.

A minute later, turned from starter to judge, Dan called out the numbers of the first and second ponies, who would go forward into the semi-finals.

The winner, predictably but unfortunately, was the one strange pony ridden by the one strange child. The pony was very nice, Dan thought, and the child very nasty — a pot-hunting outsider, a heavy user of the whip, with heavy hands and a lumping seat and expensive jodhpurs and ignorant parents. Dan and both Hadfield sisters had been looking out all day for excuses to disqualify the child in a series of events. But she was winning everything. She had a cluster of the rosettes — 'Albany Gymkhana, First" — which the Hadfield sisters bought annually at moderate cost, for this high point of their year. Dan was sorry for the local children riding the old bored riding-school ponies; he was very sorry for the pretty silver-grey pony of the rich outsider.

Dan was sorry for himself, too. He wanted a nap and he wanted a drink, and it was hours before he would get either. He wanted the nap because he had been out before dawn attending to the pheasant snares he had set the previous midnight at the edge of the Medwell Court preserves. He wanted the drink because, after the misty cool of the dawn, it had turned into one of the blazing days that Dorset gets in the middle of September.

The Hadfield sisters — the very old Miss Trixie, the scarcely less old Miss Hettie — looked equally thirsty. The wrinkled faces were scarlet; their grey hair draggled damply over their temples. They wore unseasonable tweed coats, collars and ties, breeches, riding-boots and bowler hats, as though they were going cubbing instead of entertaining their own pupils at their own riding school at their annual gymkhana.

Dan himself had also dressed up in daft clothes suitable for the occasion. He wore baggy corduroy breeches, the leather gaiters his father had worn before he turned from gamekeeper to poacher, and a wide flat tweed cap in startling checks. He kept a wheatstraw between his teeth as though it were a pipe, in dim recollection of an illustration to a Surtees novel. His mother thought it a desperate humiliation that he should be seen in public looking like an antique pad-groom — he who had been a scholarship boy at the Grammar School, who could have been assistant manager of the Milchester bank by now, who had so grossly betrayed and disappointed her by following in his father's wicked footsteps. But he thought it right to dress the part — any part he was playing, including bank manager — and he thought overdoing it was a fault on the right side. He always wore these breeches, gaiters and cap when he helped out at the Albany gymkhana.

The gymkhana was always on the second Sunday in September, just before the children went back to school. It made a climax to the summer holidays, the Hadfields thought. It was something to aim at, through the riding lessons the children had all holidays. If it clashed with other events in the world of horse sport, this scarcely mattered, since nobody involved in it would ever be involved in an event of greater pretension. It was a family affair.

It was not strictly a closed event. Outsiders were permitted. The Hadfield sisters had handbills printed in Milchester, advertising the gymkhana, and stuck them in the windows of newsagents in half a dozen villages. They were pleased if a few local children came on their own ponies and even carried away a few of the resplendent rosettes. The thirty or forty pence they paid to enter each event helped to meet the cost of the rosettes, and of Dan Mallett. They set a standard, too, for the riding-school youngsters on the apathetic riding-school ponies; they provided healthy competition; they made a change; they were new faces, of which the Hadfields saw very few; their families swelled the tiny crowd.

What nobody wanted or expected was a gigantic lemon-yellow horse-box to thunder up to Albany Farm, with a girl groom and a thousand-pound pony; what nobody wanted or expected was a cross-faced overweight townie thrashing the animal and winning everything and being petted by overweight townie parents in a silver BMW.

The box was terribly in the way. It took up half the bit of rough grazing the Hadfields called a car park. Dan had a chance to inspect it, briefly and wonderingly, before things got properly going; he saw that it accommodated the girl groom as well as the pony. It was magnificent. He did not get a chance to inspect the girl groom closely, owing to the pressures of the gymkhana and the greater pressures of the Hadfield sisters. From what he fleetingly saw, she was pretty magnificent too. She had short hair, almost white, and green eyes, and a turned-up nose; she wore jeans and a T-shirt, which she nicely filled. She was the sort of girl Dan liked. (The sort included tall brunettes, plump redheads, Orientals, twittering shop-assistants, opulent barmaids, foxhunting young ladies from county families, and assistant matrons at the Medwell Priory School.) He thought the girl groom was in the wrong company, but he did not have leisure to brood about it.

The expensive grey pony won the final run of the bending race. The rider grabbed the rosette from Miss Trixie Hadfield and jammed it on her bridle. She cantered over to her family's car, making the hot pony hotter still. She heaved herself off and looked round impatiently. The girl groom hurried up, took the pony's reins and led the poor brute away. It was the classiest pony Dan had ever seen, in all his years of doing this ridiculous job, among the rag, tag and bobtail which lolloped round the paddocks at Albany Farm. It was a beautiful mover. The girl was, too. Dan considered her behind as she walked away from him, the tight jeans pushed elegantly this way and that with her movement.

'Dan!' barked Miss Hettie Hadfield. 'Have you fallen into a trance? The potato race starts in three minutes. All entries to the collecting ring immediately. Wake up, boy!'

Dan sighed and picked up the megaphone. He was over thirty, but he was a boy to the Hadfield sisters. He supposed he always would be. They were not stupid; they did not mean to be insulting; it was simply that nothing changed their attitudes to anything. He'd be young Dan Mallett — 'Wake up, boy!' — until he had a long white beard. He wondered why he liked the arrogant old ladies. But he did like them.

He bellowed through the megaphone in the accent he used to the Hadfield sisters and the other nobs of the neighbourhood — the broad, treacly, antique Wessex which made them think he was quaint yet reliable. He bellowed: 'Tatty race d'start en thray mennets! All antries d'cam t'collecken rengl'

There were a few derisive chuckles at the unschooled commonness of his accent from the Milchester shopkeepers whose children came to the riding school. Dan wondered if he was overdoing the accent as grossly as he sometimes did out of mischief or overanxiety. He wondered if the megaphone was overdoing it for him. But it was still a fault on the right side. It made these shopkeepers feel wonderfully superior; and it made him, in other guises, almost totally unrecognizable to them.

The strange grey pony was not in the potato race. Its owner picked her events. This one called for dexterity on the rider's part as well as nimbleness on the pony's. Another grey was entered, not dissimilar to the outsider at first glance, but as different as a partridge from a peregrine if you knew where to look. Its head was coarser, its shoulder straighter, its chest narrower but its loins thicker, its neck heavier but its quarters lighter, its expression gloomier, its movements clumsier. It was well ridden by a farmer's twelve-year-old son, but he could hardly make it go, and then hardly make it stop. It was no good.

'Money down the drain,' said Miss Trixie Hadfield to her sister, watching the pony's lumbering career up the paddock towards the bucket of potatoes at the far end.

'Not much money,' said Miss Hettie Hadfield, a sharp defensive note in her voice.

'Too much,' snapped Miss Trixie. 'Said so at the time. You would bid for it. Now look at it.'

'A-ben a new poany jest a-botten, ma'am?' asked Dan, speaking his broadest parody of a rural accent in order to disarm any resentment they might feel at his interruption. It usually did disarm resentment, because people thought he was a kind of pixie, permitted audacities denied to the sane and adult.

'Milchester market last Thursday,' said Miss Trixie. 'My sister bid up and up, although I said a hundred times if I said it once — '

'You said it at least a hundred times, dear,' said Miss Hettie with dangerous gentleness.

They quarrelled constantly, with each other and with the rest of the world. But any quarrel with the rest of the world found them as united as Siamese twins.

Dan called out the numbers of the first three in the potato race. The grey from Milchester market was not among them.

As Dan crossed the paddock immediately afterwards to make things ready for the relay race, he was half blinded by a flash of reflected sunlight from the car park. Another shiny expensive car had nosed in there, a huge fawn Mercedes like Major March's at Medwell Court. Dan was surprised that Major March was putting in an appearance at the gymkhana — Ascot races in a company box was more his mark.

Dan hung on his heel for a moment, thinking of the fat young pheasants he had taken home ten hours earlier, from the Major's woods. He was disinclined to come face to face with the Major just now. The Major's head keeper knew an uncomfortable lot about Dan. He was longing for a chance to nab him.

But, to Dan's relief, the man who got out of the car was nothing like Major March. The latter was typical, to Dan's mind, of the new false gentry who had taken over the countryside — city gents, financiers or industrialists, the estates owned by their companies or run as tax-fiddles: pop-eyed men who wore tweeds like fancy dress, tried to buy local popularity, and employed a vicious stamp of gamekeeper. The man who climbed out of the Mercedes was the Major's age — late fifties — but in other ways very different. He was tall and powerfully built. He looked as active and healthy as Dan himself, though he was twenty-five years older, inches taller, and a good seven stone heavier. Instead of the false tweeds Major March would have worn, he had on khaki cotton pants and a blue cotton shirt, short-sleeved and open-necked, which showed brown muscular arms and a solid pillar of neck. They were absolutely sensible clothes for the weather and the occasion — just such clothes as Dan would have worn if he were not dressed up as a riding-school groom. The man carried a Panama hat. This was also sensible, but Dan would not have followed him there, unless someone like Major March had left a Panama hat lying around . . .

The newcomer was fair. He had a strong-featured craggy face. Dan guessed he would be attractive to women. The face looked capable of severity, perhaps of violent anger, but at the moment the man was looking round with a sort of childish delight. He smiled. The smile grew and grew as he stared at the swarm of ponies and children, then at the comfortable old brick of Albany Farm and its outbuildings.

He turned to say something into the car, which Dan did not hear. Two fair-haired children scrambled out of the huge car, a boy and girl, about ten and twelve. They also looked pleased with everything they saw — more astonished and delighted than the humdrum scene deserved. It was as though they had never been to the country before — never seen ponies — never seen an old farmhouse out of sight of any other building than its own barns and stables.

Dan wondered for a moment if they were foreigners, to gape with such joyful amazement at such familiar things. But they looked intensely English. They were not local people. Dan knew every rich man for many miles round, and all about him — being a full-time poacher and part-time burglar obliged him to do so — and this man was unknown to him. The people were strangers, tourists. But it was odd. Albany, set in a loop of the river, was so deeply buried in the countryside, so far from a main road, so hard to find, that no stranger went there without a good reason and a good map.

Probably they were staying with a local nob, as it might be Major

March; the children had seen a notice of the gymkhana in a village shop window and had asked to come. No doubt that was it — something as ordinary as that. It was still odd that they looked as though they had found the crock of gold at the end of the rainbow, at a scrubby little gymkhana on a small farm.

Dan put the attractive family out of his mind as he struggled to get things ready for the relay race, pursued by the impatient screeching of both Hadfield sisters.

Libby Franklin walked Hector, the lovely grey pony, round and round in a paddock near the car park. She had taken off his saddle and put on a sweat-rug. He could not be given the deep drink and haybag he wanted because Melissa Cox would be riding him again in a few minutes, flogging him over little jumps or cantering in tight circles in her avid search for rosettes. Libby could do no more for Hector than keep him moving gently while the sweat dried from his neck and shoulders.

Melissa was ruining his mouth and his temperament, just as her parents were ruining her. It was an awful shame. Not about Melissa — Libby didn't give a damn about Melissa, although usually she liked children – but about Hector. He was a super pony. He deserved better. The irony was that Libby had found him for the Coxes, as well as the chestnut left behind in a paddock in the village. The chestnut had a cut, an over-reach. Melissa had wanted to ride him today in spite of his evident discomfort; Libby had managed to persuade Melissa's parents that the pony ought to be rested. She had used the argument about the pony's value, about protecting their investment. The argument had worked, but it had put Melissa in a thoroughly ugly mood. She was taking it out on Hector.

The chestnut was an old pony. Hector was only a five-year-old, but fully made by an experienced child, one of a family who knew what they were about. Libby herself had been brought up with ponies, by an expert but impoverished mother. Libby's choice of career had been virtually dictated by this. Her education had been sketchy in other directions — a good school had been beyond them, and the local in Bedfordshire had utterly failed to interest her in anything. Now, at twenty-three, Libby still had a schoolgirl passion for horses, all kinds of horses. Liking children too, her idea was to work in — perhaps one day to run — a riding school. A better one, she hoped, than this rabbity little Albany place. But she had no qualifications, from the British Horse Society or anybody else, so she had to take what jobs she could. The job with the Coxes was by far the worst yet. She'd leave the moment she found something different.

It was a shame, she thought, about Albany Farm, as well as about Hector and Melissa and herself. The little old farmhouse was sweet, and the stable yard could be patched up and painted and made very smart. The children, the pupils, seemed to be all right, too, just ordinary children. But the ponies were really grotty, and so were the two old bags who owned the place.

The oddity was the groom, or whatever he was, who trotted about the place in gaiters like an old-fashioned chauffeur, and covered his head with a huge tweed cap that made him look like a bedroom candlestick upside-down. He chewed a straw, like Soapey Sponge in the pictures in the only books Libby ever read. He had amazingly bright blue eyes in a small brown face. Libby had not seen him at close quarters, but even at long range those eyes shone like lamps. They had followed her about a bit. Libby was well-used to being followed by men's eyes, especially when she was wearing tight jeans and T-shirt, but not by such wide, innocent eyes of cornflower blue. His voice, which Libby heard from time to time through his loud-hailer, was deep and slow and sweet, like separated honey. His accent came out of the Ark. Libby had not realized that people still talked like that, even in remote country places. But she, like the Coxes, came from near London, from the commuter belt. She had never been deep into the West Country before.

It was one good thing about the Coxes, bringing her down here — or rather sending her off in the palatial box and following in the BMW. Melissa wanted to get some value out of her expensive ponies, and the gymkhanas near home were too hard to win. There were other rich children there with high-class ponies, and some of them could ride. So the Coxes toured round tiny little gymkhanas like this one, and Melissa had a vast collection of meaningless rosettes. She and her parents stayed in luxury pubs. Libby pigged it in the box, on the groom's bunk behind the cab.

At least they paid her pretty well.

A family, Libby saw, was watching her and Hector from the edge of the paddock by the car park. Her circuit of the paddock took her close by them. It was a middle-aged man and two children. Probably his children, from the look of them all, although he looked old to be the father of young children. They were a goodlooking family, fair, with strong regular features. The man was still attractive in a Kurt Jurgens way. The children had no eyes for her — they were staring with open yearning at Hector.

'He's beautiful,' said the little girl, as Libby and Hector came by.

'He's the most beautiful thing I've ever seen,' breathed the boy, who was a bit younger still.

Libby smiled and stopped. Hector flapped his ears, bored but still sweet-tempered in spite of Melissa Cox.

The children asked politely if they might stroke the pony's neck. They did so nervously, tentatively. Libby was sure they had never been so close to a pony before.

Libby chatted idly to the father (he was indeed the father) while the children cooed at Hector and stroked him with growing confidence.

'London kids, I'm afraid,' said the father, who had a pleasant enough voice with a slightly Cockney accent. 'Nice for them here. It's what I plan for them, all this . . .' He gestured vaguely round at the farmhouse and the crowded paddocks.

'Dad,' said the little boy, 'can I whisper?'

The father grinned, made an apologetic face to Libby, and bent down so that his son could reach his ear.

After listening to a passionate whispered message, the father straightened and said, 'I don't know. You'd better ask the young lady. You know how to ask politely. The worst she can do is say no.'

'You ask, Dad.'

'No, Al. It's something you want — you make the effort.'

He was a much better father, Libby thought, than Mr Cox.

Blushing, desperate with eagerness, the little boy asked to be allowed to sit on Hector's back.

'Of course you can,' said Libby immediately.

The father lifted the boy on to Hector's back. Libby showed him how to hold the reins while she kept a grip of the bridle.

'If you feel unsafe, Albert,' she said, 'just hold on to his mane. He won't mind.'

'Not Albert,' said the boy. 'Albany.'

'Good gracious,' said Libby. 'What a weird coincidence.'

'Not at all,' said the father, smiling. 'I was born here. My folks had this place for generations. Yeomen farmers, freeholders. My Dad had to sell in the 'twenties, but I wanted to — dunno — keep a kind of link with it. Al's name is the link.'

'He gets teased about it at school,' said the girl, whose name was Althea.

'I don't mind. I'm proud of my name,' said Albany. ''Specially now I've seen what I'm called after.'

'What a shame your father had to sell,' said Libby to the man.

'Yes,' he said shortly. 'Everything went wrong after that. I finished up in Dr Barnado's.'

'An orphan? What happened to your parents?'

'Died soon after we got chucked out of here. First her, then him. I haven't forgotten, nor will forget. I wanted these two to see the place they sprang from.'

'They ought to get it back.'

'They're going to.'

Libby glanced at the father, startled at the quiet certainty in his voice.

2

There was a break, but not long enough for Dan Mallett to get either the drink or the nap he wanted. He decided he could use the few minutes best by taking a closer look at the pale-haired girl groom. He started across the grass to where she was leading the grey pony round. He saw that she was giving a ride to one of the kids who'd got out of the Mercedes. Evidently the child had never ridden before. The grey pony would be a wonderful schoolmaster for him, so responsive and so smooth in his action. Maybe the owner of the Mercedes would make an offer for the pony. It often happened at gymkhanas, as it did on the racecourse and in the hunting field. It was why a lot of farming families went in for gymkhanas, to flog the ponies they bred and broke.

Who ought to buy the grey pony, Dan thought, was the Hadfield sisters. Swap it for the useless animal they'd just acquired . . .

He thought, as he thought nearly all the time, of the daunting sum of money he himself needed. An idea began to form itself in his mind. It was hazy; it was frightening. It meant talking to the girl groom, and it meant talking very carefully and delicately to Miss Trixie Hadfield.

The grey pony would be much better taken away from that fat, cross-faced little pig who did everything with the whip.

Dan quickened his stride towards the pale-haired girl and the family from the Mercedes.

'Congratulations on your victor ludorum,' said a gentle voice behind Libby — a voice with a trace, but only a pleasant trace, of Dorset accent.

She stopped Hector and turned.

To her complete amazement, the gaitered groom stood there with his cap in his hand.

He was looking at Libby with unabashed, unselfconscious approval. His blue eyes undressed her, but they did it in the nicest possible way. She realized with a start that he was an intensely attractive man. He was quite as attractive as the big fair Londoner, but in the opposite way. The children's father would be someone to rush to for comfort, for safety. This small brown man with untidy brown hair would be someone to take on your lap and cuddle . . .

And well he knows it, thought Libby, looking at the wedge-shaped face, unlined but deeply weatherbeaten, the narrow brown hands, the straight nose, the guileless and mesmeric blue eyes.

'That loud-hailer thing does extraordinary things to your voice,' she said abruptly, feeling herself blushing, to her annoyance.

'Goes with the gaiters,' he said mildly. 'Have you come far with your juggernaut?'

'Only from Ighampton this morning,' said Libby.

'Back there tonight?'

'No, I'll be in the village here, Medwell Fratrorum.'

'Ah? Parked on the cricket pitch?'

'No. Someone called Mr Potter is letting me park in his drive. He's a friend of Mr Cox, my boss. Then we're going back to Esher tomorrow. That's where they live.'

The blue-eyed man nodded. He patted Hector's neck with an experienced hand, and looked at his legs with an experienced eye.

'Six-year-old?' he said.

'Five. How did you guess?'

'I'm half an animal myself.'

Libby led Hector back to the waiting little girl, Althea, and her father. The girl had called that it was her turn, and her brother had reluctantly agreed. The slim, soft-voiced man in gaiters walked with them, continuing to inspect both the pony and herself. His astonishing blue eyes, when he looked at her, were just as expert and appraising as when he looked at the pony. She became intensely, unusually, aware of her bosom bouncing slightly in the tight T-shirt as she walked.

Al was lifted off, Althea lifted on. She was a thoroughly nice child; they both were. The father had come a long way, Libby thought, from Barnado's to the Mercedes that Al had pointed out to her. It would be lovely if he could buy the farm back, his family's old home. Maybe the crazy old women would sell.

As Libby walked off, Althea clutching the pony's mane and grinning like a kitten, a scream rent the air: 'Libby!'

A small army was advancing towards the pony. In front, waving her whip, stumped Melissa Cox. Behind her came her fat parents.

'What d'you think you're doing?' screamed Melissa. 'That's *my* horse. Who said you could let other people ride it?' she screamed at Althea, 'Get off! How dare you?'

She hit Althea with her whip. It was only a tap. Althea was startled but not hurt. There was no mark on her bare leg. But Libby lost her temper.

'You nasty little selfish spoilt bitch,' she said, 'you don't deserve a good pony.'

'That's enough!' came another scream. It was Mrs Cox. In a voice of hysterical outrage, echoed by her fat obedient husband, she sacked Libby. It was out of hand, immediate. They'd send her the money she was due. She could get her things out of the box and go where the hell she liked. The Cox family would have nothing more to do with her after she had talked to Melissa like that.

'Fine,' said Libby, still furious. 'Suits me.'

She lifted Althea off Hector. Melissa led the pony away.

'I'll drive the box to the Potters' myself,' said Mr Cox crossly to his wife. 'After this slut gets her rubbish out of it.'

Dan had been watching impassively, effacing himself but missing nothing. He was pleased that the girl groom had spoken her mind to the cross-faced child. Her voice was just right for saying, "You nasty little selfish spoilt bitch' — a cool, clear, posh voice, like the voices of the Hadfield sisters. She went higher in his estimation, and she'd been pretty high before.

The big fair man from the Mercedes stepped forward. He said to the girl, 'I'm really sorry. We were the cause of that.'

'It doesn't matter,' she said. 'It would have happened tomorrow if not today.'

'Funny thing is,' said the stranger, 'it just may have been a bit of

luck for all concerned. I've been looking for someone who knows
about things I don't know about. I'll learn, but not overnight. Listen — I think I told you I want to get clear out of London, bring
the kids up in a place like this. With what they need, ought to have.
Animals, fresh air.'

'Yes?' said the girl.

'I'm ignorant about a lot of things, though I was born on a farm.
I don't know how to choose a pony, or how to look after one. I
don't even know what they eat. But I want ponies and I want them
soon. Know anything about dogs?'

'Yes,' said the girl, not surprising Dan.

'Good. I want dogs. I want a dozen dogs. I want the kids to have
their own dogs. I want pigeons and hens and geese, and maybe
goats and donkeys. I want the kids to have all the things I was
cheated out of. But I don't *know* enough, not yet. I've always, all
my life, found it paid to get help when I needed it. It has paid too.
Paid all along the line. Good business principle. I'm applying it
now. This is not charity, it's business. I'm partly responsible for
that fracas just now, but that's not why I'm saying this. Whatever
that toffee-nosed cow was paying you, I'll match it and better.
Starting this minute. Okay?'

The girl looked as astounded as Dan felt. At the same time,
presumably she did need a job. And presumably she saw, as clearly
as Dan saw, that this was a rich man with nice kids.

The girl looked undecided, almost flummoxed. Of course it was
terribly sudden. But Dan thought that, after she'd recovered herself, she'd say yes.

She said yes.

The kids gave yelps of joy. They'd fallen for the girl in a big way,
since she'd given them rides on the pony and spoken kindly. The
big man grinned, shook hands with the girl called Libby, and intro-
duced himself as Eddie Birch.

The name jangled a faint bell in Dan's mind, But he could think
of no reason why he should have heard of a rich businessman from
a distant city.

Dan heard urgent shouts from the Hadfield sisters. He trotted
away from the Birch family and their new employee, and started
calling entries to the collecting ring for the next event.

Dan was interested in the scene he had just watched, in the ways the different people had reacted. The possessiveness of the fat Surrey girl, shouting 'It's mine!' like a baby and hitting out like a baby. The self-importance of the fat Surrey mother, who wouldn't take plain speaking from anyone poorer. The obedience of the fat father. The splendid, immediate loss of temper by the girl called Libby. They had all given themselves away, in that small moment of crisis. They had announced a lot about themselves.

So had one other. Dan had glanced from the fair girl, briefly, at the big man called Eddie Birch, just after the Surrey girl had hit Althea with her whip. He saw an interesting reaction there, too. For a moment — for the fraction of a blink of an eyelid — a look of the most naked and passionate fury had filled that big handsome face. The calm grey eyes glared red; the calm features were contorted into a mask of hatred. And then it went — disappeared so completely and so quickly that Dan wondered if he had imagined it. And afterwards Eddie Birch had spoken sensibly and kindly.

The big man had a temper, but he also had the most remarkable self-discipline.

Dan helped clean up the mess. Miss Trixie and Miss Hettie were having one of their usual, interminable arguments, which slowed things up. The argument was the more bitter because they were both very tired after the gymkhana. They were very old for such an exhausting day — Miss Trixie seventy-five, Miss Hettie seventy-two. They were arguing about the other grey pony, the one Miss Hettie had bought at auction in Milchester market. Miss Hettie defended the pony. Her position was untenable, but she would not budge from it. Neither of them ever did.

Miss Trixie said she would give anything to exchange the useless grey pony for the other which had won all the prizes at the gymkhana.

Later, catching her alone, Dan delicately pursued the matter. He speculated about the value of the strangers' grey, about the difference in value between the two.

He thought Miss Trixie knew what he was talking about. But she was much too downy an old bird to come right out and say so.

Dan asked her, just as a point of interest, exactly how much she would give, in cash money, to exchange the two grey ponies.

Miss Trixie looked at him sharply. 'Two hundred pounds,' she said.

'Ar, ma'am, ma'am,' said Dan, his voice like obsequious treacle, his accent as broad as the paddock. 'A-ben sax hunder pun differ atween they tew horsen.'

'I daresay,' said Miss Trixie. 'But I haven't got six hundred. What I've got, in cash, by me, is two hundred. Sale of that old mare, that old Rosebud. Harry Simpson gave me cash for her, and my sister hasn't *seen fit* to drive me to the bank yet.'

'Hum,' said Dan.

He was quite sure the old ladies had more than two hundred in cash by them. They did everything they could in cash, to avoid the vexations of tax and VAT. Dan also knew that Miss Trixie wouldn't stick to it, like her sister. They were both as obstinate as mules, as the new grey pony they'd bought.

'Hum,' said Dan again, inconclusively.

Miss Trixie looked at him, frowning; but he wandered away to gather up some drifting litter.

Dan bicycled gently home as the sun was touching the stubble fields to the west. The plough was advancing over the countryside after the harvest, strips and squares of dark brown cutting into the pale gold. The new-turned earth looked cold and dead, but really it was teeming with life, with snakes and worms and mice and voles and moles and the grubs of all kinds of insects. That was why gulls followed the plough exactly as they followed a ship, hoping for titbits. Even closer, almost on the ploughshares, went the pied wagtails. They ran along the ridges, bright black and white showing up vividly on the brown, then popped downwards into a furrow, or fluttered a yard and settled, tails bobbing up and down like something in the window of a toyshop. Dan always wondered why wagtails walked and ran, like Christians, when other small birds hopped. His father had called them 'dishwashers', because they liked bouncing and bobbing in shallow water. They liked fresh plough just as much, because they ate all the bugs and grubs in the new-turned earth. They were perky little birds, show-offs, swanks. Dan liked them.

A short way from the mouth of the Albany Farm drive, the river looped towards the road, then looped away again towards Willie Martin's river woods below Yewstop Farm. A heron stood on the river bank, not ten yards from the road, staring down into the water, still as a willow-stump. It showed how little the road was used. Aware of Dan, the heron took off, knowing quite well that a water-keeper would have shot it. It had a curious way of getting started. It bent at the knees, then straightened its legs suddenly and jumped off the ground. At the same moment it threw its head and great long neck and sword-sharp beak forward. It was shifting its centre of gravity, turning from something vertical into something horizontal, in order to get airborne. For a moment it looked ridiculous, oafish. After a couple of heavy wing-beats it was moving, climbing, properly on the wing; and then it folded up its neck and tucked its head into its shoulders. It had three personalities — the motionless, disciplined hunter; the awkward and clumsy great fool trying to get off the ground; and the powerful, graceful flier. Like people, Dan thought, showing up well, then badly, then well again in a new way.

That big man called Eddie Birch might be a bit like a heron — the iron self-control to wait patiently for the moment to strike, and then the big, sharp, heavy weapon to strike with. He could be graceful enough too, speaking smoothly and humming over the country in his huge car. Did he have moments of awkwardness, helplessness? If not, he was unique.

Dan had to climb a moderate hill after passing Yewstop Farm. He freewheeled, at walking pace, down into the river valley again. There was mist on the river. The mist was rising quite sharply as the sun went down and the warmth left the air, so that the riverside trees seemed to be rooted in mist. Dan noticed a distinct drop in temperature as he whispered downhill into the misty valley.

Huge flocks of peewits tumbled and cried over the new plough. Parties of late swallows and martins were travelling southwards. Wasps snarled about the ripening pears in the trees, where blackbirds had bitten holes in them. Michaelmas daisies, monotonously purple, were the only colour in the cottage gardens.

Soon the first frost would come. Dan was worried about the effects of cold and damp on his mother's arthritis. He left the road, and followed the track to the cramped little cottage, once a game-keeper's, at the edge of the Priory woods.

His mother was feeding the blue-marble bantams by the cottage door when he put his bicycle in the shed.

'No need to bother with that, old lady,' Dan said, alarmed at the fatigue in her face, as white and wrinkled as crumpled tissue-paper.

'Couldn't know when ye'd be back.' she said. 'That hen d'want her supper, that Gloria.'

'She's a greedy one,' Dan admitted.

'All ben well wi' they Hadfield 'immen?'

'Well enough. There's a girl groom got a new home, and a pony needs one. I'm seeing to that tonight.'

She glanced at him, with eyes as sharp as Miss Trixie Hadfield's. She saw quite as much, or more. She sighed, threw the bantams the last of their corn, and hobbled painfully indoors.

That sigh expressed everything — everything she thought all the time, looked so often, and very seldom said — her unappeased dis-appointment in the life he had chosen. Every day he felt guilty about the way he had let her down. But all day every day he thanked God he had left the bank — peeled off his dark suit and white collar and his little black shoes, jumped off the broad straight dreary highway of success, wriggled into the secret, teeming woods and ditches where he belonged — paced away his ballpoint pen, his engagement diary, his calculating machine, pulled out from their hiding-places his father's snares and nets . . .

He watched his mother's retreating back, the painful la-boriousness of her movements, her reliance on the rubber-tipped stick. She was not one to moan, but that arthritic hip was paining her more and more. They could put in a plastic one nowadays. It freed you from pain, let you jump about like a good 'un. Admiral Jenkyn in the village had had it done, and caught trout as well as any of them. Of course he'd paid, been to a posh private clinic in London. But they could do it in the hospital, on the Health, practi-cally for free.

'Not to me they can't,' said old Mrs Mallett. 'Not in they yuge wards, wi' sneerin' doctors an' nurses like a flue-brush.'

Nothing would shake her refusal to go into a public ward in a National Health hospital. She was quite as mulish as the Hadfield sisters.

But the operation grew more and more necessary. Dr Smith said so, and Dan, who trusted almost nobody, trusted Dr Smith on the illogical but convincing grounds that he cast a dry-fly so beautifully.

The operation was necessary. She wouldn't have it done on the Health. Therefore she must have it done privately, like Admiral Jenkyn. That would cost at least £1,200, and the longer they left it the more it would cost, like everything else. Therefore Dan must get £1,200, or a bit more. He'd gone only a short way towards this monstrous figure. He needed more, soon.

Therefore he must remove the silver-grey pony from the box in Mr Potter's drive. He had never stolen a horse before — nothing larger than a roedeer, and he never thought of poaching as stealing. But the more he thought about it, the more he saw it as a moral duty. Not only for his mother's sake, but also for the pony's. People could say what they liked about the Hadfields — their obstinacy, snobbishness, quarrelsome, extreme reluctance to pay bills — but they did look after their animals. No pony could have a better home than Albany. It would be heaven for the grey after that fat family from Surrey.

A moral duty. But Dan gulped at the thought of the night ahead.

Dan fed his dogs in the kennel and then let them out for a run — Pansy the bad-tempered old pointer, Nimrod the sleek black lurcher, Ruby the crossbred Jack Russell terrier. They were not pets (although Nimrod and Ruby thought they were) but working dogs, as necessary to Dan as snares and shotgun. They were fed well, carefully and differently; their food would have been expensive if Dan had bought it.

With the dogs back in the kennel, Dan climbed into his little pigeon loft over the shed. He topped up the feeding-hoppers for the blue-laced Satinettes. He gave them a mixture of Tasmanian peas, wheat, and Cinquatina maize. This would have been expensive too, if it had not come from the storeroom of the Medwell Court pigeon stud. The girl who looked after the Major's pigeons was a particular friend of Dan's.

Dan watched as the Satinettes scuffled on the floor round the hoppers. Each bird ate what it wanted and no more; after eating, they all waddled across the floor of the loft for a drink of water. They never returned for more food. They were moderate, sensible; they looked after themselves. Dan thought, for the thousandth time, how much people could learn from the rest of creation.

Having fed animals and birds, Dan fed his mother and himself. His own appetite was prodigious; it was amazing, even to himself, that he stayed so light and slim. He watched, worried, as his mother pushed away the potatoes on her plate, and ate only a little of the roast pheasant. She said she had not done anything all day to give herself an appetite. It was true, and it was heartbreaking. She had once been as active as Dan himself; her paper-white face had been as brown as his.

At 10 o'clock Dan helped his mother up the awkward little stairs to her bedroom. At 10.30 he gave her a hot drink and an aspirin, and tucked her up.

She looked at him broodingly from the pillow. There were new lines of pain in her face; there was the familiar disapproval in her eyes.

'What ye up to tonight, then?' she asked.

'Just a bit of horse-dealing.'

'At poachin' time? Market ben at four in the mornin'?'

'This one is. Special market.'

'Mus' be.'

'Matter o' moral duty.'

'Ho! Ye don't know what they words d'mean.'

'Good night, old lady. Sleep well.'

She said she would, but he knew she wouldn't.

He had, at last, the nap he had wanted all day. He stretched out on his bed, half dressed, having set his mental alarm for one in the morning. It woke him half an hour early, which surprised him. Usually it was reliable within five minutes. He realized that his own tenseness was responsible. He was slightly aghast at what he was doing.

He pulled on dark trousers and sweater, and lightweight boots with rubber soles. He pondered for a moment, wondering what he needed. There'd be tack for the pony in the box, but he had to get into the box. He took a jemmy, a screwdriver, pliers, and a pencil flashlight. He thought about noise. He stood in the middle of his tiny, tidy bedroom, scratching his head absently with the screwdriver. He regretted his inexperience in this field. After a minute he took two pairs of heavy woollen socks out of a drawer, a length of strong nylon fishing-line, and a clasp-knife.

Just before one he went softly downstairs and out. He locked the cottage door and put the key in a gap between bricks behind a drainpipe. The dogs clamoured excitedly; Ruby the terrier thought she was coming. He quietened them urgently, wanting to disturb his mother as little as possible. He set off across country on foot, towards the village.

The Potters lived at the Old Mill, a picturesque conversion on the river at the edge of Medwell. Mr Potter was an insurance broker, nearing retirement, spending three days a week in London. Mrs Potter had once been on the stage, people said; she had a self-conscious voice and purple lipstick. They were horrible people, rude to the girls in the village shop. This removed any trace of compunction from Dan's attitude to them. Mr Potter had a small collection of antique clocks. Dan, doing odd jobs in the house, had studied the clocks, the layout of the building, and the burglar alarm. Though only a novice burglar, he had his eye on the clocks. The problem was transport. Clocks were heavy, awkward; they had to be carried carefully, unlike a sack of silver candlesticks. Dan's idea was to use Mr Potter's own Volvo Estate — though he had never had a licence or taken any test, even in his years at the Bank, he was a skilful and dashing driver. The project of the clocks was a good one, a sound one. But it was a project for another time.

Avoiding the roads — he used them at night no more than a fox did — Dan went fast, without hurrying. He knew every yard of his way. It was a chilly night with heavy mist on the low ground. Dan was glad of the mist — it baffled the eye if lights went on, and it deadened sound. He was glad of his heavy sweater, too. He passed through a crowded, busy nocturnal world of noisy owls, silent foxes and badgers, mysterious woodcocks secretly feeding on the mudflats. Half nature was as busy at night as Dan was, doing the same things, hunting and surviving.

Dan got to the Old Mill at a quarter to two. The mist was clammy. The night was very dark. He went delicately up the grass beside the asphalted drive. It was a good thing the Potters had this ugly black drive instead of gravel. It was a good thing they had no dog. At least, they had not had one a week before. But people suddenly acquired dogs, which was a lesson Dan had once painfully learned.

A mountain loomed blacker in the blackness — the horse-box. It had been backed into the drive, so the ramp faced the house. This was bad — a surprise, and thoroughly bad.

Dan crept up to the box and laid an ear to its side. There was no sound — no sleepy breathing, no shifting of feet. His heart sank. It seemed the pony had been taken out of the box and put in a stable or paddock. It was a good thing to have done. Sensible ponies lay down at night, so they wanted space. It was unnatural to keep one all night in the narrow cell of a horse-box, confined by the partitions, tied up by the head. Because it was unnatural, Dan had assumed the dreadful family would have done it. But it seemed the pony was out. The Potters had neither stables nor paddock — only a patch of over-manicured garden — but there were paddocks nearby, and the pub two hundred yards away had stabling. It made things easier, if he found the pony. But it might be very difficult to find. And in the morning it was going back to Surrey with the fat, cross-faced owners.

Then Dan heard, through the metal wall of the box, a gentle whistling. It was air in the nostrils of a pony. There was no noise quite like it.

Dan padded softly to the back of the box. Another shape loomed behind the box — a car. Dan groped for the radiator grille. It was not Mr Potter's Volvo. The grille was contained in two ovals. It was a BMW. The family was here. They were staying with the Potters. They were friends of the Potters — exactly the sort of friends the Potters would have. Of course they were here — nothing could more easily have been predicted. It made no difference one way or the other, as far as Dan could see. What was important was that the

BMW was not so close to the box that the ramp could not be lowered.

Dan was thankful that he had had a good look at the box in the field at Albany. The lower half of the back hinged down to form the ramp; above was a pair of doors. The doors lapped over the top of the ramp, and they locked.

Dan stood still and listened. The mist felt like wet flannel. There was no light or sound from the house. There was no noise at all, except the distant scream of an owl in the yews of the churchyard. Dan reached up for the door-handle, groping over the mist-dampened metal in the dark. He thought the doors would be locked. His fingers found the chrome-plated handle. It felt cold and wet. It turned. It was not locked. They had not bothered to lock it, the box being so close to the house. Perhaps they had not adjusted to not having a girl groom to look after their property.

The girl, the one they called Libby, had removed herself and her things. None of the family would be sleeping in the horsebox. It was highly unlikely that they had hired someone else so soon. Nobody would be in the box, except the silver-grey pony.

Dan opened the doors. The hinges were well oiled; the doors opened silently. He groped for, found, and pulled out the pins that held up the ramp. He lowered the ramp, settling the bottom end silently on the drive. He did not want to use his flash until he had to. He crept up the matting of the ramp into the box. His fingers found a rubber-covered chain hooked across from the wall to a partition. Beyond the chain he felt the warm rump of a pony.

He blinked his flash on the pony for a split second. It was the wrong pony. It was a chestnut, penned into the narrow stall. The grey was beside it, in the next stall, in a sweat-rug. Both ponies wore halters; the halter-ropes were tied very short to rings in the metal wall in front of them. They could hardly move.

Dan was shocked. The chestnut must be mad with boredom. The grey pony had been working hard. It must have been longing for a roll and a lie-down. These people didn't deserve a good pony. They didn't deserve any animals at all. They were not fit to keep them.

Dan squeezed up beside the grey pony to its head. He began to fumble in the dark with the knot of the halter-rope on the ring. The pony was quite placid. He was half asleep. The tricky part was to come.

Lights blazed — two brilliant beams, from close behind the horse-box. It was the headlights of the BMW. At the same moment its horn blared. Lights came on in the house. A dog barked.

3

There were shouts. Doors slammed. Feet pattered.

Dan was trapped.

But, crouched in front of the grey pony, he thought he was invisible. The floor of the horse-box was higher than the headlights of the car. Though the pony was narrow, he was narrower still. His face and hands were hidden; the rest of him was dark, camouflaged against the dark inside wall of the box. They might not spot him immediately. They might not think he was actually in the box, not all at once. But they would come and look soon, unless he provided a diversion. The Potters knew his face.

If he could not be seen, by the same token he could not see. He heard men's and women's voices, and the screeching of the child — both Potters, the three others. Feet crashed about in the garden. Mr Potter wailed about his plants. The fat child screeched that her ponies were safe. She wanted to go back to bed. The dog barked like a fool.

Dan pulled the cuff of his sweater down over his right hand. He hid the skin which, though browned by the sun, would show pale and sharply visible in the car's headlights. He slid the camouflaged hand across to the chestnut's head. His hand was now hidden by the chestnut. He freed his fingers from the sweater, and untied the knot of the halter-rope. The chestnut tossed its head, realizing it was free.

Dan dropped to the floor of the box and crawled towards the ponies' tails. He was in shadow on the floor; he kept his face on the floor, inhaling straw and dust. He was likely to be trodden on, but the ponies were not very heavy. There was a fair amount of muck amongst the straw; this was no time to worry about little things.

He raised an arm, with infinite caution, using the partition to hide it. He unhooked the chain from behind the chestnut pony's rump. It fell with a small crash against the side of the box. The noise was audible even over the shouting of the people and the barking of the dog.

'What was that?' called a woman.

None of them knew. None of them had been watching the back of the chestnut pony at that moment. None of them noticed that the chain had disappeared from behind his rump.

Dan slithered to the ponies' heads again, rose to a crouch, and pushed the chestnut backwards. The pony jibbed. He was frightened. He did not like the glare of the headlights or the shouts of the people. He suddenly went backwards fast. He skittered backwards down the ramp and into the front of the BMW, his halter-rope trailing. He reared, then lashed out behind, panicked at backing into the car, panicked by the glaring lights. There was a clang as one of his shoes hit a wing. He lashed out again. Glass tinkled, and there was only half as much light flooding into the horse-box. The pony bolted into the flower-beds.

Mr Potter wailed.

'Catch him!' screamed the fat child.

Dan heard the pony's hooves on the drive in front of the box. The pony bolted down the drive and out on to the road. Feet pattered after him, presumably in bedroom-slippers or gum-boots. Voices receded. Apparently they had all gone after the chestnut pony. The thought of Mrs Potter chasing a runaway pony, in the middle of a misty night, in her dressing-gown, was astonishing. The dog, still barking, ran off with the people.

Dan ventured a peep over the grey pony's shoulder. But he was dazzled by the remaining headlight of the BMW. There could have been an army beside the car, invisible to him. He opened the groom's door in the side of the box, and peeped round that. There was nobody in the drive. They had all gone out and along the road. Dan listened intently. There was no sound near at hand. He was alone, unless someone was waiting in silence, waiting in a sort of ambush. This was clearly possible. It was clearly sensible, but people were apt to behave less than sensibly when marauders disturbed them at two in the morning.

What had happened, obviously, was that the dog had heard or otherwise sensed him, in spite of his care. Probably the dog had come with the fat Surrey family; it had been in their car all day. No doubt it wanted exercise, even at this hour, as badly as the chestnut pony did.

The dog had woken somebody in the house. That somebody had softly woken others. Someone had crept out, reached in a hand through the open window of the car, switched on the lights and pressed the horn. Something like that. Now they had all rushed away after the bored and frightened animal.

All?

Dan slid out of the groom's door, and dived into shrubs beside the drive. There was no outcry. No one had seen him. He went round the back of the car, and to the driver's window. He switched off the headlight, finding the right switch after trying several others. The drive was still lit by the lights from the house.

Dan realized for the first time that the front door of the Old Mill was wide open. Light flooded out from the hall into the garden.

It came to Dan, with something like a shock, that this was a night for clocks as well as for ponies.

He stood still, listening intently. There were distant shouts, hardly audible through the blanketing mist. He couldn't tell if they had caught the pony. One or more might be back quite soon. He didn't need long.

As quiet as a spider, trying not to make any overconfident assumptions, Dan ran to the side of the house. He went along it to the front door, and slipped in. Once again he paused, motionless, listening. All he heard was the ticking of several clocks in the study off the hall. They were calling an invitation.

Knowing exactly where to go, Dan found two lightweight suitcases in a box-room. He took a broad strap with a buckle from another suitcase, an old-fashioned heavy leather one. He did not pause to search the bedroom or any of the upstairs rooms. Time was of the essence.

He ran downstairs. Yet again he froze, standing in the hall, listening. Nothing. He went into the study. There were nine clocks. They all had pendulums, mesmerically swinging, some visible through glass panels. The pendulums hung from strips of highly-tempered steel. Before the clocks could be moved, the pendulums must all be unhooked and packed separately, or the works could be damaged. Dan knew little about clocks, but he had taken the precaution of learning this much from a jeweller in Milchester when he first made his plans.

Dan put four clocks in one suitcase, packing them carefully, padding and protecting them with a blanket. He put four more in the other case. He packed away the pendulums. He left what looked to him the least valuable clock, not as consolation to Mr Potter but because he had no room for it. He was careful to touch nothing except the clocks he took, the blankets and the suitcases.

He slid out of the front door with the utmost caution. He put the suitcases down beside the car. He threaded the broad leather strap through the handles of the cases, and did up the buckle.

He ran up into the horse-box. He had one further precaution to take. He hoped there was time for it. He switched on his pencil flash and held it in his mouth to free his hands. He lifted the pony's feet, one by one, as though to look at the shoes or pick them out. The pony was well used to this, and almost lifted his feet before Dan asked him to. Dan pulled a thick woollen sock over each foot. He tied the socks over the coronets of the hooves with bits of his nylon fishing-line. The socks would not last long, but they would muffle the hoofbeats for a while.

Dan undid the chain behind the grey pony, untied his halter-rope, and backed the pony down the ramp. The pony went cautiously because of the darkness, but he was a kind, tractable animal and did exactly as Dan asked. His feet made little noise, cuddled in the thick woolly socks. In the light from the front door the socks looked utterly ridiculous.

Dan had intended to find a bridle and ride the pony away. He could have crossed any country. The pony was not very big, but he was up to Dan's weight. But now a bridle was unnecessary. Dan had not a saddle-pony but a pack-pony. He folded the sweat-rug so that it formed a pad behind the pony's withers, then heaved the suitcases on to the pony's back. They hung each side, the strap between. The folded rug protected the pony's back from being chafed by the strap or the cases.

The pony would come to no harm. The clocks would come to no harm, well packed in blankets, carried by a pony at a walk.

Dan led the pony through the garden and out of the back gate by the river. The pony walked along cheerfully. If he disliked the unfamiliar burden he showed no signs of it. It was probably far pleasanter to be carrying two suitcases than a fat Surrey girl with a cutting-whip.

Dan had a long way to go. He had to go by his own cottage before he went to Albany. For the first part of the journey he had to go slowly and carefully, not because of the sure-footed pony but because of the clocks. He did not go right to his cottage, because of waking the dogs and disturbing his mother. He led the pony instead into the Priory woods. He went along a ride which he knew intimately. The pony, trusting him, followed confidently, even through the pitch-dark dripping wood. Dan tied the pony to a tree, and heaved the suitcases off his back. He undid the strap, and pushed the suitcases under the roots of a fallen willow. With his pencil flash in his mouth he camouflaged them thoroughly. They should have been inside polythene bags, but they would not be in the woods long, and modern lightweight suitcases were pretty waterproof. The clocks would be all right for a day or two, unless there was a flood.

Dan emerged from the wood. As soon as he was on firm ground he took the remnants of the woolly socks off the pony's feet. They had stood up surprisingly well. They were no longer any use to Dan, which was a pity, as his mother had knitted them. If he was to make a business of horse-stealing, he thought, he must come by a set of the leather boots which you put on a horse's injured foot to keep the frog clean.

He made much better time the rest of the way to Albany. He rode part of the way. The pony was docile enough to be managed in a halter. He did not ask too much of the pony after its distressing day at the gymkhana. It was only a little after five when he led the pony into the Albany stable-yard.

He knew the stables as well as he knew his own shed. There was an empty loose-box at the end. He put the pony into it, took off the halter, and gave him a brick of hay from the loft above, and a bucket of water from the standpipe in the yard. The pony had a long drink. Dan refilled the bucket.

All this took a very few minutes. He still had time to take the other pony, the useless one from Milchester market, all the way back to the village. He planned to ride it there, and to let it go in the Potters' garden.

Of course, even the fat Surrey people would see the substitution. But their story would sound very odd to the police. They might even not be believed. Meanwhile the Hadfields had a receipt for the price of their pony. It would only carry a bare description — size and colour — and the description would do very well for the Surrey pony.

And the Surrey people would go back to Surrey. And the daughter would go back to school — no doubt an expensive school where the right-minded kids would detest her. And the girl groom had gone off with the Birch family, to buy ponies and dogs and hens for them.

All the Hadfields had to do was to keep their new grey pony out of sight for a few weeks, then say it was the one they had bought at the market. It would be the only 13-hand grey pony in their string. It *could* only be the one they'd bought at Milchester market.

The whole thing, in fact, was beautifully tidy: just as long as Dan could get the Hadfields' grey into the Old Mill garden before dawn.

He guessed the pony was out. He took the halter into the nearest paddock, and blinked his pencil flash at the sleepy ponies there. He went into the next paddock and immediately found the surly grey pony with the common head. He caught him, put the halter on, and led him towards the gate.

Once again he was bathed in glaring light. It was a big electric lantern. Miss Hettie Hadfield was holding it. Under her other arm she held a 16-bore shotgun.

'Let that pony go, Dan Mallett,' she said coldly, 'before I blow a hole in your tummy.'

Dan had known Miss Hettie all his life. He had ridden the ponies at Albany when he was a schoolboy in return for mucking out and grooming. Now he was the occasional odd-job man of the place; patching fences and mending hay-racks, as well as the factotum of the annual gymkhana. His knowledge of Miss Hettie made him let go of the pony's halter immediately. She had at least twice loosed off the old 16-bore at people she thought were horse-thieves.

'I couldn't sleep,' said Miss Hettie, 'worse luck for you. Heard a clatter in the yard. Pinched something out of the stables, have you?'

'A-ben spaken,' said Dan anxiously, adopting a voice like clotted cream, 't'yer saster, ma'am —'

'She wants to get rid of this pony, eh? To spite me? I see. Typical. I said it was a grand stamp of animal and I say so still. Beauty's more than skin deep. She never could judge horse-flesh. Thinks she can, and then she's pig-headed about it. Hasn't admitted she was wrong about a horse since she backed Tudor Minstrel in the Derby. Found excuses for herself even then.'

'Ben a prablem,' said Dan apologetically. He tried to explain that there was now a grey pony too many at Albany.

Miss Hettie was not impressed. Dan was not sure she fully understood; he was sure that he was not going to be allowed to take the Milchester pony away. He said, despairingly, that he must return the Surrey pony to the Mill.

'What, and lose your money?' said Miss Hettie sharply. 'Whatever you're doing for my sister, I bet you're not doing it for nothing.'

'Hum,' said Dan. The £200 was another necessary step towards the £1,200. He wanted it badly, and the sooner the better.

Miss Hettie was as sharp as her sister — as sharp as his own mother.

Time was racing by. There was hardly enough left, after this bother, to get either pony to Medwell before dawn.

'Ben a tangle,' said Dan, thinking with dismay of the hazards and complications which faced him.

'All of your own making,' said Miss Hettie severely, 'yours and my sister's. Now go away, like a good boy. If anything happens to my pony I shall know who to report to the police.'

Dan was not *really* frightened of the shotgun under Miss Hettie's arm. He was sure he could have knocked it out of her grasp. Even if he didn't do that he could run away. To fire the gun, Miss Hettie would have to put the electric lantern down. Other people might fire a shotgun from the hip, one-handed, but the old lady would need both hands. Dan could run away, behind the lantern, clear of its beam. She would have little chance of hitting him, in the dark, running. He had got away from much better shots than Miss Hettie, angry gamekeepers with 12-bores. Sometimes they were protecting their pheasant-poults and sometimes they were protecting their daughters; either way they were shooting to hit, and they missed.

But running away solved no problems. If he ran away with the pony, Miss Hettie would report him to the police. Dan might feel a sort of ancient loyalty to her, but she felt none whatever towards him. In her eyes, he was in a conspiracy with her sister to cheat and humiliate her. He was a common horsethief. She would shoot him if she could, and report him to the police if she couldn't. She had said she'd do so; she'd keep her promise; nothing in the world would stop her.

If Dan went away without the pony, there was a grey pony too many at Albany. But, for the moment, it was what he had to do.

Miss Hettie escorted him off the farm, her finger on the trigger of the shotgun.

Dan walked, suddenly intensely weary, along the narrow, high-banked drive from the farmhouse to the Medwell road. Once Albany had had all the land he was walking through, all the land within the loop of the river as far as the road which crossed the neck of the loop. It was a small farm, even then, not quite a hundred acres, not enough for a decent living. The old ladies had years ago sold a cowman's cottage and three acres at the other end, to some weekend people. The people had a right of way through the farm, right by the house and the stables. They were a quiet little couple, childless, no trouble, going sensibly and carefully when they drove past the stables. The Hadfields spoke of them with snobbish disdain, but really they were pretty good neighbours. Dan had done a few jobs for them. He liked them moderately, although they spoke a different language from any of his languages.

Two-thirds of the rest of the farm, sixty acres, had been sold only last year. The Hadfields needed the money. The land was not much good to them. It had been let go long before Dan's time, even before the war, by old Colonel Hadfield. He had given up trying to farm it, if he ever had tried, and planted a lot of trees for pheasant-covert. His idea was to let the shooting and make a lot of money, but it didn't work out. There were never any pheasants there. If there had been, Dan would have known about them. He might not have taken them, but he would have known about them.

Fred Mortimer had bought the land. He was the biggest farmer for miles round, and he bought any parcel of land that came on the market. In time Fred would have cleared it and made it pay. But before he could get round to doing so, to using his men in the slack season, he had burned himself up in his own barn.* His executors were trying to sell the land, Dan had heard, or let it pending a sale. It would be dear at £400 an acre; £24,000 would certainly secure it. Dan thought the executors might have a job finding a buyer for sixty acres of scrubby woodland. Planning permission to build was most unlikely. Another snag was that Albany Farm kept a right of way through the land. It had to — going through Fred Mortimer's bit was the only way to get to the farm and the cottage beyond, owing to the loop in the river. The whole piece was like the letter U, almost the letter O, with the river coiling round it.

As he trudged, Dan pictured a lark's eye view of the farm. It was really almost an island. The reason was the slowness of the river and the flatness of its valley. A faster river would have cut a straighter course. But this river was amazingly serpentine. It was like several other West Country rivers Dan had seen — most like the Nadder, perhaps, which meanders from Tisbury to Wilton in a series of lazy horseshoes. There were places on the Nadder where you could dig quite a short ditch and turn a hundred-acre peninsula into an island. It was the same, in there.

Albany was a peninsula, and the neck of land between the two arms of the river at their nearest was scrubby, overgrown woodland. The road beyond was little used. It all made Albany a sort of secret place, very isolated, utterly secluded. That, no doubt, was why Colonel Hadfield had bought it when he retired from India and the army. Dan's mother remembered the Colonel as a man who lived for privacy, horses, salmon fishing, and his two daughters, in that order. Maybe, Dan reflected as he trudged up the lane, his passion for privacy was the reason his daughters never married. Or, to

---

* This horrible episode — with which Dan Mallett was closely concerned — is described in *Fire in the Barley* (Constable 1977) by the same author.

put it another way, why they had married horses instead of husbands.

He came out of the drive by the little blind turning on to the road. It was a very minor road, with peculiar cambers. It was a mile east to Yewstop Farm and Willie Martin's river woods, two miles on from there to the village. Milchester was eight miles the other way, westwards. The nearest place was the little cluster of cottages called Medwell Zellaby. That was two miles north, but it might have been two hundred, since it was beyond the river and the extensive marshes which bordered it there.

Dan left the road and struck across country, going the direct way home like a February dog-fox after clicketing.

The Hadfields, he thought, would soon be too old to live by themselves in such an isolated place. They were already almost too old to look after all those ponies and run the riding school. But it was the life they loved, the only life they knew. They loved the place, too. The stables looked ramshackle, but they were sound. The grazing was well cared-for, Miss Hettie grinding to and fro on the tractor, pulling a harrow or muck-spreader. The fences were a weird, pinch-penny patchwork, but they kept the ponies in. And they had the house exactly as they liked it — exactly. Dan guessed as their father had liked it. They squabbled about everything, but in the end things came out as they wanted.

Dan wondered about the Hadfield sisters' future. He wondered about his own future, too, with one pony too many at the farm.

The sky and the mist were milky when Dan got home. Millions of new cobwebs were drenched in the heavy dew. There were burrs all over his trouser-legs, as though the burdocks wanted to spread their seeds in his bedroom.

His mother called, after he had quietened the dogs and let himself in. He ran upstairs.

'You smell nex' kin to muck-heap,' she said.

Dan realized that he did; he remembered his slow-worm crawl along the floor of the horse-box.

'Contact wi' quadrupeds,' he said. 'Like a drop o' tea, old lady?'

When he had made it, he found her looking at him with worry as

well as disapproval. He reassured her. He convinced her that everything was all right. But, thinking of the two grey ponies, he had
difficulty convincing himself.

He had a light first breakfast, a nap, then a heavy second breakfast. He was sweetly asleep at the hour when, a few years earlier,
he would have trotted into the bank in Milchester to begin his daily
damnation.

Dan bicycled to Albany after his second breakfast, feeling perfectly
refreshed but not perfectly happy.

They had found the silver-grey pony in the loose-box, of course.
Miss Trixie was delighted, Miss Hettie disdainful, in spite of the
rosettes it had won. She continued to proclaim the merits of her
own grey pony, on account of her refusal to retreat from the position she had taken.

Miss Trixie gave Dan £200 in cash — a collection of dirty ones,
fives and tens, which suited him admirably.

'If I am asked,' she said, 'I shall, of course, simply say that I
bought the pony from you, in good faith.'

'Nay, ma'am,' said Dan, appalled. 'Ye bot un t'Milchester market!
ye got the paper for t'prove un! Grey poany, thirteen hander — receipt d'truthful describe thicky poany, ma'am!'

'That would be perfectly satisfactory,' said Miss Trixie, 'if my
sister would consent to part with her brute. As you know, she will
not consent to do so. I advise you against trying to remove the animal, in view of the mood Hettie's in.'

'Ay,' said Dan, thinking of the 16-bore and of Miss Hettie going
to the police.

'I feel perfectly easy in my conscience about having that new
pony here,' said Miss Trixie, 'although some people might think it
odd.'

'A mossel odd,' Dan agreed.

'I have paid for it. I am a purchaser in good faith.'

'Hum,' said Dan.

'What is more important is, I have removed it, with your help,
from a completely unsuitable home.'

'I thoughted sim'lar,' said Dan.

'I am doing the pony a kindness. I regard it, in fact, as a moral duty.'

Startled at this echo of his own words, Dan nodded, and came near to tugging his forelock. He was not at all sure if Miss Trixie was truly convinced of her moral rightness. Like almost everyone connected with horses, in Dan's experience, Miss Trixie had flexible morals, especially when buying and selling ponies. Probably the Colonel had been the same, when coping Arabs and Kabulis in India before the first War.

Miss Trixie's moral flexibility, Dan thought, would make her careful. She was nobody's fool. She must see as clearly as Dan did that the lovely grey pony must be kept under wraps for a while.

At least, he hoped she must.

On this not altogether satisfactory note, Dan bicycled to Medwell by way of the Old Mill. He sped by the Mill at unusual speed, not wishing to come face to face with the Surrey family who might remember his interest in the pony. But they had gone — the box and the silver BMW. He wondered if they had caught the chestnut, and, if not, whether he might catch it and sell it to someone.

He glanced back into the Old Mill as he sped away into the village. A police car, coming from the Milchester direction, turned into the drive.

Clocks. They'd come about the clocks, more than about ponies. Fretting about ponies had put the clocks out of Dan's mind. If they were anything but clocks, they'd be best left where they were for six months, then taken quietly to the shop. But you couldn't leave clocks under a root and then expect to get a fair price for them.

Getting them to the shop would be tricky. If he was stopped and searched . . . And he would be, if he was seen carrying two bright new suitcases with something heavy inside. Or any other heavy burden. Every policeman for miles around would know about the clocks pretty soon, if he didn't know already. And a good many of them knew Dan's face. He'd never been convicted of anything, but he'd come terribly close to it. There was a Detective Chief Superintendent, with a sharp red face like a fox, who knew Dan rather well; there was a Sergeant, with a big white face like a Hereford bullock, who knew him rather better. All the same, the clocks couldn't stay where they were.

Dan stopped his bicycle by the General Stores in the middle of Medwell Fratrorum. He pondered the problem, one foot on the kerb to prop himself. A bus stopped in front of him — a private bus, a bus full of noisy little girls in round blue hats. It had met the girls at Milchester station, and was taking them to Medwell Priory, lately a mansion, now an expensive school. The children poured out of the bus into the shop, to buy chocolates and sticky sweets in order to assuage the misery of going back to boarding-school. They sounded like a cage full of budgerigars. They were saying it was unfair, stinking, rotten, foul. Because they came on the train, they got back to school hours before they needed to — hours before the girls whose fathers brought them by car.

Dan's problem was solved.

4

Dan propped his bicycle against the window of the shop. He walked to the front of the bus. As he hoped, the driver was a stranger, probably a Milchester man.

'Message from Miss Cavendish,' said Dan importantly.

'Who's she?' asked the driver.

'Headmistress o' the Priory School.'

'Ow. Who are you?'

'Caretaker there.'

'Jake Collis is caretaker there.'

This was true. Dan had not expected the driver to know it. He said, 'Jake's off queer, wi' a rumblin' stummick.'

'Ow,' said the driver. 'What's the message?'

''Nother train to be met, a special. On'y half a dozen girls on it, plus baggage.'

A dozen of the little girls had come out of the shop, chewing their purchases. Some climbed into the bus; some stood staring at Dan and listening to the conversation.

'Okay,' said the driver. 'I'll drop this lot an' go back into town.'

'I 'spec,' said Dan, 'your passengers'd liefer you took 'em into town, met the rest, an' delivered the whole boiling together.'

All the passengers, except one who felt sick in the bus, shrilly approved of this idea.

It was all one to the driver.

The rest of the little girls climbed on to the bus, carrying Dan with them.

Dan said to the driver, as the bus thudded into motion, 'Mind if we go round a piece? I ben tol' to take some clobber into Milchester.'

It was still all the same to the driver, and to all the little girls except the one who felt sick.

Dan directed the driver to his own cottage, but stopped him out of sight of it by the end of the track. He said he'd be three minutes. He raced into the woods, hauled the suitcases out of their hiding place, brushed the earth off them, and staggered with them to the cottage. He ran into the cottage and upstairs, calling noncommittally to his mother in the parlour. He pulled off his clothes. He dressed up as an assistant bank manager, in neat dark suit, neat white shirt with semi-stiff collar, dark tie, navy-blue socks with crimson clocks, and neat black shoes with a high polish. He very rarely wore his old prison uniform, but sometimes it was right. For selling antique clocks it was right.

His mother looked at him wistfully as he passed the door of the parlour. This was how she liked him. He was dressed up as her dream of him. She might even feel renewed hope. He hoped not.

He hurried back to the bus, lurching a little between the two heavy suitcases.

'Some three mennits,' said the driver. 'Liker thirty.'

'Eleven minutes and forty-four seconds,' said a very small girl with a very large wristwatch.

Dan grinned at her. He stowed his suitcases among dozens of others in the back of the bus. He sat low in a seat, half covered by friendly little girls. Some said they liked his smart clothes better than his other clothes, but there was wide disagreement about this. Dan said he was not really a caretaker, not all the time. He said he was really in the Secret Service.

Two miles out of the village on the Milchester road, a line of cars was stopped. There was a police car. A policeman in uniform was flagging the cars down. Other policemen were talking to people in the cars, and one of the cars was being searched. Dan saw open suitcases.

Dan sat lower in his seat, the girl with the fine wristwatch on his lap. The Sergeant like a Hereford bullock glanced at the bus. The police waved the bus on.

'Lookin' for drugs, likely,' said the driver.

'Why? Do policemen like drugs?' asked the girl with the watch.

The bus thundered on into Milchester.

Dan asked the driver to stop at the corner of West Street. He heaved his suitcases carefully down. He stood waving to his new friends until the bus disappeared round the corner. He made a mental note to stay well clear of Medwell Priory, at least for a term or two.

He wondered for a moment what would happen when the bus got to the station. It didn't greatly matter. It wouldn't bother the driver; it wouldn't bother the little girls, who had had an extra hour of freedom.

Dan humped the suitcases down West Street to an antique shop called 'The Box of Delights'.

There were some silver candlesticks in the window. Dan peered at them uneasily through the dusty glass. He was relieved to see that they were not the ones which he himself had sold to the shop three weeks earlier.

He pushed in, jangling the bell over the door. The proprietress rose from a rocking-chair to greet him — a middle-aged woman with a strong jaw, arty clothes, and a pink chiffon bandeau round her head.

'Good morning, Mr Barnett,' she said in a baritone voice.

'Good morning, Miss Huxtable,' said Dan, in his best banker's manner. He put down the suitcases, and said ruefully, 'Obliged to dispose of some more of my household gods.'

'Times are hard.'

'Times are very hard. Fortunately I've recently been left a small collection of antique clocks . . .'

'Ah. May one peep?'

She examined them. She said she was not an expert on clocks, and could only price them approximately.

'I take it,' she said casually, looking away from him, 'that your wishes in regard to the sale of your silver should apply to these clocks also? You want me to use, ah, similar discretion?'

'Yes, please,' said Dan. 'I still don't want my friends to know that I'm broke. It's the best way to lose friends.'

Miss Huxtable laughed understandably. She went along with his fiction, because it made their relationship more comfortable, and because it put her in the clear (or somewhere near it) if anyone was inquisitive about the clocks. She had no idea who or what he was, but he supposed she saw quite as clearly as Miss Trixie Hadfield did.

She showed how clearly she saw when she suggested keeping the clocks, wrapped in their blankets, in the smart new suitcases. Dan agreed to throw in the suitcases, which were not initialled, for a few pounds extra. He said he had more luggage than he needed, which was true, as he needed none whatever.

Miss Huxtable said the clocks would probably go abroad. She gave him £200 on account. It was not nearly enough, but he was selling in a buyers' market. The money was in used notes of mixed denominations, like Miss Trixie's money. It joined Miss Trixie's inside the lining of his blue banker's coat.

Dan said he would call again, when another lot of bills forced him to sacrifice another lot of inherited treasures. Miss Huxtable said he was always welcome with merchandise of good quality, especially if not crested or monogrammed.

They shook hands and parted affably.

Dan walked to the Market Square and took the public bus back to Medwell.

A police car was parked by the village shop when Dan went there for his bicycle. Out of it climbed the Sergeant with the big white Hereford-bullock face.

'You,' he said, 'you, Mallett. You're dressed up bloody grand. Ben to a funeral, you thievin' little bastard?'

'Ay,' said Dan, grinning oafishly. He regretted being seen by the police in his banker's clothes, preferring them to picture him as a half-witted yokel.

'Know anythin',' said the Sergeant, 'about a grey pony?'

Dan shook his head, letting his eyes widen and his mouth fall open.

'We fancied you might,' said the Sergeant. 'First off, 'cos you're the biggest villain unhung, poach or pench anythin' soon as look at un. Second, 'cos we knows you need a pile of money for your ma's operation, same like Dr Smith tol' us weeks back. Third, 'cos we knows you knows all about ponies an' such, seein' you ben years wi' those Hadfield ladies. Fourth, 'cos we knows you seen the pony, an' looked at un partic'lar yesterday, all day yesterday.'

'Hum,' said Dan uneasily. 'A-seed a grey poany, 'tes true.'

'Whoever took the pony,' said the Sergeant, 'likely took a load o' clocks at the same time, val'able antique clocks. Whoever that was, he knowed about the clocks aforehand, and knowed about the house where they was. Which you did, seein' you done jobs for Mr Potter.'

'A-ben up Potter's,' admitted Dan.

'Ben an' looked round an' went back last night.'

'Nay! A-ben slapen like a babby, a-ben 'at tired.'

'An' your ma will swear you never left the house. We got eyes on you, bloody Mallett, big eyes we got. We're lookin' for a stolen pony, an' a set o' clocks, an' we're lookin' at you very close.'

Dan grinned oafishly again, having no reply to any of this.

Four hundred pounds in banknotes rustled in the lining of his coat when he moved. The Sergeant might search him. He had done so before. He was entitled to do so, since he had reasonable grounds for suspecting Dan. Dan wanted to run away, very fast, in any direction. But he would be running straight into prison if he did.

The Sergeant stared at him. He stared back, trying to keep panic out of his face. Seconds dragged by. Dan thought the Sergeant was trying to decide what to do.

The Sergeant looked at his watch, grunted, and got back into the police car. Dan bicycled away. He was seriously alarmed.

Miss Huxtable at 'The Box of Delights' would get a police circular describing the clocks. She'd keep quiet, no doubt, because she'd want to get her £200 back with maybe 1,000 per cent profit. But, if pressed, she'd describe 'Mr Barnett' — she'd have to

The police were practically bound to go to Albany sooner or later, to ask about the grey pony. One grey pony — either one — was covered by the receipt from the Milchester auctioneers. But if there were two grey ponies, one an obvious beauty . . .

Dan hurried home and changed into working clothes. He hid the £400, with his other savings, in a polythene bag in a rabbit-hole.

He gave his mother her meal, and saw with renewed dismay how little she ate. He was dismayed also at the thought that the Hadfields might use their new pony. It was fit. It was by far the best animal they had. It would be cruel, as well as wasteful, to keep it locked up for weeks in a loose-box. Secluded as Albany was, people went there. A few people would be going there, even though the children, the pupils, would soon be back at school for the autumn term.

Meanwhile, Miss Hettie Hadfield was determined to keep *her* grey pony, to vindicate her judgement. She would be all the more determined after catching Dan in the middle of the night. A thing like that put her blood up. It would be doubly a point of honour with her, to keep the pony she'd bought.

'It's a muck-up,' said Dan, aloud.

'Nay,' said his mother, playing with her vegetables. ''Tes nice.'

But she still left most of her meal on the side of her plate.

Dan bicycled to Albany at 3 o'clock. The pony muck-up was what had to be sorted out. He hoped to influence the situation in some way, though it was hard to see what way. The best he could think of was to buy the grey pony, the Surrey pony, back from Miss Trixie Hadfield. It went terribly against the grain to lose his hard-earned £200, but it was the best he could think of.

Half a dozen children were at the farm, being given a lesson by Miss Hettie Hadfield. Some were emotionally saying good-bye to the riding-school ponies. They got very fond of the ponies, apathetic as most of the animals were. Miss Hettie's Milchester grey was not being ridden; it was out in a paddock with some others. There was no sign of Miss Trixie's new pony. Miss Hettie was dressed in jodhpurs, tweed coat, and bowler hat. She looked very hot and out of temper.

The Morrisons drove through the farm, the weekend couple who had the old cowman's cottage. Dan was surprised to see them going to the cottage instead of away from it, on a Monday.

'Taking a week's holiday,' explained Mr Morrison, who had a thin sandy beard and a high, whinnying voice. 'Recuperation after the stress of a metropolitan summer.'

They wanted some odd jobs done, which Dan promised to try to see to during the week.

Miss Trixie came out of the house, dressed exactly like her sister and, like her, carrying a whip. Dan trotted up to her and asked to buy the grey pony back. She flatly refused to sell.

'For one thing,' she said, 'I like it. For another, where's your money?'

'Ye knows a-got un,' said Dan.

'I don't know any such thing. You might have lost it or spent it, a feckless boy like you. I wouldn't dream of selling without cash on the nail, not to you. I wouldn't dream of selling that pony anyway.'

Dan offered her more than the £200 she had paid him. He offered her £50 more: then, miserably, £100 more.

Miss Trixie was not interested. They were not so very short of money since selling the sixty acres to Fred Mortimer. They had acquired a good pony cheaply. Miss Trixie was happy with things as they were.

'That pony,' she said, 'will be looked after properly for a change. I can't think why you want it, anyway. You've got no stabling, no hay, nothing. Are you thinking of setting up a riding school? In competition to this one? You can hardly expect me to help you. Or do you see yourself reselling? Who to? How do I know it would go to a good home? No, no, you took my money and glad to get it — that's the end of the matter. Don't bore me about it again.'

At this moment a large Mercedes whispered up the track from the road. It stopped near the farm. Out of it got the big fair man from London, his two attractive children, and the pale-haired girl groom.

Libby Franklin had been treated with more kindness in twenty-four hours than she had met in six months from the Cox family in Esher. Al and Althea were warm-hearted, impulsive children, mad to have their own animals, mad to live in the country, mad to learn all that she could teach them. Their father was gentle with them, but without silly indulgence. He was obviously besotted about them, but he didn't make the mistake of spoiling them.

'Difficult not to,' he said to Libby, after the children had gone reluctantly but obediently to bed in the Red Lion in Milchester. 'Especially since their mother pushed off.'

'Oh,' said Libby. 'I wondered. How sad.'

'Yes, very. I don't really blame her for leaving me. Definitely dodgy, leaving the kids, but she did have grounds for leaving me. I didn't play around, mind. It wasn't like that. I never had time or energy left over after a day's work. I didn't have time or energy for her. She didn't want to go to nightclubs every night, not that we were in what you might call the nightclub bracket, not in those days — but she did want *some* attention. I used to come home, late, all hours, and flop out flaked in a chair. Not much fun for her. She was much younger than me, as you might guess, looking at the kids. So . . .'

Libby nodded. He must have worked, to get from a Dr Barnado's home to that Mercedes, the best rooms at the Red Lion, the big flat he described in Bayswater, the boarding-schools the children were going to. Libby thought he was tough. She guessed he'd taken a short cut or two. It was difficult to blame him, starting so low, and with those children to make a good life for.

She warmly approved of his plans for the children. He asked her what she thought, almost anxiously. She reassured him; he seemed to value her reassurance.

The children warmly approved of his plans, too. They were wild with excitement when he asked them, at breakfast in the hotel, if they'd like to live at Albany Farm.

'I can offer them a good price,' he said. 'More than a fair price. Not like their Dad did to mine.'

'I hope it works,' said Libby sincerely.

'It will,' said Eddie Birch.

'Will you stay with us, if it does?' asked Althea.

'Not if,' said her father. 'When.'

'If you want me to,' said Libby.

They did want her to, all three of them. They needed her. Libby found it nice to be needed.

After lunch, a glorious and very expensive lunch, they all drove out to Albany. Al was thrilled at the thought of going to live at a place with the same name as his own.

'Like the Duke of Devonshire,' suggested Libby.

'Except that he lives in Derbyshire,' said Al's father, laughing, as he drew up by the farmhouse.

'New pupils?' said the older of the two old ladies who ran the place.

'Could they have a lesson?' said Eddie Birch. 'Why not? I didn't think of that.'

The children were agog to have a lesson. They ran over to the other old lady, who fitted them out with riding hats, and helped them on to small, fat, elderly ponies.

'A curious time to enroll,' said the first old lady severely. 'Don't they go to school?'

'Ah, we start as we mean to go on,' said Eddie Birch.

'If you didn't come here for riding lessons, Mr er, why did you come?'

'My name is Birch.'

'Mr Birch.'

'Mean anything to you?'

'No.'

'Remember Will Birch?'

'Should I?'

'Had this place.'

'We have had it for half a century, since my father purchased it.'

'It was my father he bought from.'

'Oh yes?'

'I was five at the time. We went to Bournemouth.'

'Ah?' said the old lady, who seemed to Libby little interested in the history of the Birch family.

Libby saw for the first time that the gaitered groom, the one she remembered from the gymkhana, was standing inconspicuously behind the old lady. He was not wearing gaiters now, and his cap was normal in size and colour. His eyes were as blue and childlike as ever. He *did* seem to be interested in the Birch family, although he was much too young to have known them at the farm here. He was interested in Libby too. He turned to look at her, as she stood by the open door of the car. He smiled in greeting — a shy smile, but to Libby's eye an extremely sexy one. She smiled back, more broadly than she meant.

'I was only five.' Eddie Birch was saying, 'but I remembered it all pretty well. Remembered it clear, ever since.' He looked round, his face thoughtful, brooding. 'It doesn't look as big as I remembered. But I don't think it's changed much.'

'The inside of the house is a great deal cleaner,' said the old lady.

Libby thought this remark offensive, but Eddie Birch did not seem to mind. He said equably, 'We cooked on coal, when we could afford it. Lit with candle and oil, when we could afford them. I daresay there was a bit of smoke.'

'The place was like a pigsty,' said the old lady. 'I vividly remember my first sight of it. I was not at all anxious to live here. My father had to spend a lot of time and money to make the place fit for civilized people to live in.'

The offensive note was clearer in the old lady's voice. Libby thought she was remembering with resentment the discomforts of fifty years ago. She was the type that learned nothing and forgot nothing.

This time her tone did get through to Eddie Birch. His face darkened, and his mouth tightened. But he kept his temper. 'I would very much like,' he said mildly, 'to come back to my Dad's place. Bring up my own children here.'

'What are you suggesting?'

'Purchase.'

'Out of the question.'

'Think about it.'

'There is no need to think about it. There is not the slightest question of our selling. This is our home. We are gentlefolk, living on our own land. We would not dream of moving away. We would not dream of allowing our home to fall into unsuitable hands.'

Still refusing to be ruffled, making a visible effort to control his temper, Eddie Birch said, 'my hands are unsuitable now, but they can learn. I inherited them from my father, like I would have inherited this place. I understand you have forty acres left of the farm, eight of woodland and thirty-two of grazing. I'm told £800 an acre is a fair price in this area. That's £32,000, pricing the woodland the same as the grazing. I believe the house has eight rooms, with kitchen and two bathrooms, main electricity, main water, oil-fired central heating. I'm advised £35,000 is a fair price. A further £15,000 for the stabling and outbuildings, which need renovation. Total of £83,000, The right of way through to the cottage would lower that figure, but I'm ignoring that aspect. I'm offering £90,000, which is considerably above the market value. In addition, I would make an offer for any or all of the stock, the ponies. I'd be guided by Miss Franklin here as to value. You'd find me generous. I would hope to buy the riding school as a going concern.

I have no idea what value to put on the name and the goodwill. Would you consider an independent valuation?'

'I will consider no part of this impertinent proposal,' said the old lady.

'Ninety thousand is only a starter,' said Eddie Birch with a smoothness Libby found extraordinary. 'Let's round it off to a hundred. Can you really turn that down?'

'Yes. Your big car and your fat cheque-book don't impress me. I was brought up with different values. Thank God I retain them. I can speak for my sister too. When we're dead you can do as you like. While we're alive we stay here. I see those children have finished their lesson. That will be £4. Good-day to you.'

'That was a tactical error,' said Eddie Birch in the car.

'What was?' asked Libby.

'Talking money like that. Coming the big spender. It rubbed her the wrong way.'

'She's an old pig,' said Libby indignantly.

'Runs in the family. Her father proper screwed my Dad. The old man had no education to speak off, no knowledge of the world. I believe he was a good practical farmer, and he worked like hell. But he couldn't make it pay. Nobody could make farming pay in those days, least of all an uneducated man with only a hundred acres. We just about got by, I believe, season after season, with a run of reasonable luck. Then he had a run of bad luck. At that moment this toff arrives, this Colonel from India with his horse-faced daughters. Waved a few hundred quid in my Dad's face, and my Dad just couldn't turn it down. He didn't have the knowledge to get a fair price, to dicker with lawyers and surveyors from London. He was screwed, cheated. We moved to a back-street slum and lived on that little bit of capital. My Dad drank most of it, having nothing to do and being miserable at leaving the farm. My Mum got pneumonia from the damp in the little house we had. It killed her. My Dad went properly to pieces. He jumped or fell off a roof. I think I have a right to the place. I think my kids have.'

'My pony was called Rosie,' said Althea from the back of the car. 'She's adorable.'

'Would you like to ride her every day?' asked her father.

'Yes! Yes! Yes!'

'Okay my pet, you will.'

Libby looked at him with surprise — the old lady's refusal had been so utterly final. He was concentrating on the road, with no particular expression in his face.

Dan was uneasy.

Miss Trixie was like a badger. Her sister the same. Once they got their teeth into something, it took a knock on the head to make them let go. Powerful jaws, too. They would never let go of Albany.

But Dan had seen the passion, almost perfectly controlled, in Eddie Birch's face. His determination and ruthlessness, no doubt, had got him where he was, all the way from being poor Will Birch's pauper son.

Dan was reminded of a philosophical question he had been asked years before at the Grammar School — what happens when an irresistible force meets an immovable object? In this case, two immovable objects?

Immovable about the grey ponies, too. Eddie Birch's visit had put Miss Trixie in a rage. She had ordered Dan never to discuss the Surrey pony again.

As he bicycled slowly home, a phrase of Miss Trixie's began to ring in his head — words she had used, defiantly and dismissively, to Eddie Birch: 'When we're dead you can do as you like. While we're alive we stay here.'

5

Adrian Morrison just couldn't turn the offer down.

He and Colette had bought the cowman's cottage six years earlier, from the Hadfield sisters. They hadn't paid much, because the cottage was in a filthy and tumbledown condition. A gardener-groom-chauffeur-handyman had lived there in the old Colonel's time. He had got too old to work, but the Hadfields let him stay on in the cottage. They couldn't, in any case, afford another full-time man, and they couldn't afford to restore the cottage.

The right of way through Albany was firmly there, in eternal black and white, in the deeds of the cottage.

Very gradually, as money and time permitted, the Morrisons had put the cottage to rights. They patched, painted, carpentered. Dan Mallett was a tower of strength. They had wiring done their first year, after the main electricity had been brought across the fields from the road; plumbing was done the second year; they got a telephone the third year; new floors, new casement windows. They tamed the three acres, carefully preserving all the trees. As far as they could they kept well away from the beehive in the corner of the patch. The bees were the Hadfields', who sometimes appeared with veils and smoke-puffers. The hive had to be in the grounds of the cottage, because anywhere else the ponies might have knocked it over. The Morrisons accepted it as a condition of their occupancy; they quite liked it being there (although they were frightened of being stung) because it seemed to give their garden the badge of rural authenticity.

Sometimes they had weekend guests who crammed themselves merrily into the tiny second bedroom — urban intellectuals like themselves, people in journalism and publishing and advertising. Everyone who came was enchanted by the privacy, the extreme seclusion. The river coiled silently round two sides of the triangular property; a rustic post-and-rail and a belt of larches divided it from the Hadfields and their riding school. The hundred acres of the farm, which was no longer a farm, cushioned the cottage from the road, which was as quiet and little-used a road as anyone had ever seen in the South of England.

It was probably a good thing that the farm was no longer farmed. Farms had smelly pigs and noisy tractors. The Morrisons had very little direct experience of such things, but they heard harrowing stories from other couples with weekend cottages. A riding school was better. It would have been better still if the Hadfields had been more friendly. But the old ladies took no interest in the Morrisons. They neither issued nor accepted invitations. They had never set foot inside the cottage after the Morrisons moved in; the Morrisons had scarcely set foot inside Albany.

Dan Mallett made up for the Hadfields. He was a godsend for odd jobs beyond Adrian Morrison's skill, as he was for so many people in the neighbourhood. He enchanted Adrian, and more especially Colette, with his treacly rural accent, his fund of old country lore, his homespun proverbs and quirky humour. Sometimes he was almost incomprehensible. Sometimes the Morrisons paraded him before their visitors as a survival they were unlikely to find anywhere else.

The Morrisons grew quite fond of the cottage, although the drive from London was increasingly exhausting. It *was* an extravagance. Adrian's income wasn't keeping pace with inflation. The rates of the cottage went up; the cost of heating it went up horribly; Dan Mallett's wages went up. Still, they would probably have hung on: but they couldn't turn down £25,000. It was far beyond the value of the property. Mr Birch knew that as well as they did.

'But I want to be sure of it,' he said. 'When you fall in love with something, you want to make sure of it. And as I'm asking for immediate possession, I feel bound to compensate you for the inconvenience.'

There was very little inconvenience, but the Morrisons allowed themselves to be compensated. They sold Mr Birch, additionally, all the carpets, curtains, bed-linen, kitchen equipment and electrical fittings, and all the furniture that was worth putting a price on. Mr Birch made no fuss about the prices. He wanted the stuff. He was a vulgar philistine, the Morrisons agreed, but it was a pleasure to do business with him.

'I'm in a rush because of my kids,' he explained. 'Nothing is worse for a child than not having a home. A firm base, like. It's a question of emotional security. You understand me? Any decision I take has got to be taken now. Not tomorrow but today, before they go off to school.'

Adrian and Mr Birch exchanged letters, written then and there at Adrian's desk.

'The whole conveyancing lark can follow after, in its own sweet time,' said Mr Birch. 'Meanwhile, these letters have contractual force. I trust you that your title is good, and there's no legal bar to the sale.'

'You can,' Adrian Morrison assured him.

Mr Birch gave them a cheque for the full amount, which was cleared within forty-eight hours.

On Friday the Morrisons drove away. They had with them their clothes, pictures, the better china, ornaments, books, the record-player and classical LPs. They left behind a cottage somewhat bare, but ready for immediate occupation.

'It's a wrench,' said Colette.

'Twenty-seven thousand pounds is balm to the wound,' said Adrian, who had never had so much money in his bank account before.

'It's hardly big enough,' said Libby dubiously.

'It's a step to higher things,' said Eddie Birch.

He said the same to the children, when he took them off to their new boarding-schools. They were a bit tense about going, Libby thought, but pretty brave. They were hugely reassured by their father's promise that they'd all get together again for the Christmas holidays, in Albany Farm itself.

'With ponies?' asked Al.

'With ponies,' said his father. 'And for Christmas I'll give you each a dog.'

'I call it a betrayal,' said Miss Trixie Hadfield to her sister. 'How *dared* those wretched Morrisons sell the cottage behind our backs?

And to that dreadful man? A self-made purse-proud bandit. I can't bear to think of him so near.'

'Knows nothing about the country,' said Miss Hettie. 'Knows nothing about horses.'

'He'll come roaring through here in his great tank of a car, honking and hooting and frightening the ponies —'

'Make them bolt. Cart some unfortunate child. There'll be a dreadful accident for which *we* shall be held responsible.'

'Put up wire on the post-and-rail.'

'Break up the drive, which *we* shall have to repair.'

'I don't like the idea of children living there.'

'Those children. Brats from the back streets.'

'Stealing things. Bothering the ponies. Vandalism.'

'Noise.'

'Dreadful noise. Wirelesses and gramophones, screams and yells. How *dared* those Morrisons be so ungrateful and treacherous?'

For once the sisters were in the fullest agreement.

'You go,' said Eddie Birch to Libby Franklin. 'You're the class. You've got the voice. I've worked on mine, but it's still out of Barnado's. You know about horses and that — you speak their language. They may take it from you like they didn't take it from me.'

'I'll try,' said Libby dubiously. 'But they struck me as obstinate.'

'Yeah . . .'

'Need you be in quite such a hurry, Mr Birch? I understand your wanting a place, and that place in particular. But they must be nearly eighty, those old ladies. They can't go on there long. You can just sit tight and wait —'

'No. That's letting them win. I won't let them win. Why should they be allowed to? Remember what they did to my family.'

'This is revenge? Because, if so —'

'Retribution. Retribution's no good on a stiff. Anyway, what do you mean revenge? I offered £100,000. I still offer it. It's far too bloody much, but that's the value I put on the place. That's how bad I want it. That and no other. It's been my dream for fifty years, to get Albany back. Especially since the kids appeared. Ten years old an' eight: it's *now* they want the kind of life I'm getting them. I don't want them London kids — pop-concerts, drugs, filth, polluted air, buildings and streets, the concrete jungle. Don't they deserve this other? All things considered? Their own ancestry considered?'

Nervously, Libby took a small hired car out from Milchester to Albany. She found the elder Miss Hadfield in the stable-yard. Miss Hadfield told her she was a traitor to her class, worse than the Morrisons because she should have known better. She almost called Libby a tart. She nearly reduced her to tears of humiliation and rage.

'You were a bit hard on that chit,' said Miss Hettie. 'Seems a nice gel.'

'I know,' said Miss Trixie unexpectedly. 'But I was still boiling with rage about those Morrisons.'

'I see,' said Eddie Birch to Libby. 'I'm sorry you were subjected to all that. It's another thing to chalk up on the slate. Something more on the debit account. I want you to move into the cottage, if that's all right with you? You needn't have anything to do with the old women. In fact, it's much better if you don't. No contact at all. No point in rows.'

'I don't ever want to set eyes on either of them.'

'Then don't you. It's a pity I can't move in there with you, but it wouldn't look right. One thing I'm going to be, in these parts, is respectable. It's important to me and vital for the kids. We'll go shopping, for food and whatever you need. You can use the telephone and so forth.'

'I won't spend all your money.'

'That's the last thing you need worry about. I sold my business two months ago — well, I won't boast about that.'

'What was your business? If you don't mind my asking?'

'Bookmaking. I started as a clerk with a little bloke who never climbed higher than the Silver Ring at Brighton. Then I got my own pitch when the War ended and I came out of the RAF. When they legalized betting shops, I raised some ready and got one. Finished with a chain of thirty-two. I thought, that's enough. Know.

why I sold? At my age, far too young to retire? To come down here and buy Albany. That single reason. Well, I mustn't stand here chatting. Since Miss Theresa Hadfield has turned us down, I must go another way about things. I must go and see the executors of a bloke who died recently.'

'Who?'

'A man called Fred Mortimer.'

In a back-street betting shop near the Kennington gasworks in South London, a big man was looking at results from Wolverhampton races. The placed horses and the odds were put up on a blackboard as the news came through on the blower. The winner was a rank outsider, a two-year-old called Mo Schmo at 20 to 1.

'That's my baby,' said the big man. 'That's my son.'

An older man, standing near him at the counter, recoiled a little. He was careful not to be obvious about this, as the big man was very big and he looked hard and mean. But his breath was terrible, unendurably rancid.

'That's my baby boy,' said the big man to the clerk behind the counter. 'My tenner on the nose. Lovely, ennit?'

The clerk gave a sick grin. He wrote the bet down as though he had laid it before the race, and handed the big man twenty £10 notes.

'And my stake,' said the big man.

The clerk, who was not a big man, handed him another tenner.

A thin dark man came out of a back office. His eyes flickered over the scene. He saw the look of satisfaction on the big man's face, the sick frightened grin of the clerk, and the 20 to 1 winner on the blackboard.

Keeping the hatred out of his voice, the dark man said, 'Phone for you, Sid.'

'Who?' said the big man.

'Your guv'nor. Calling from the country, from a box.'

The big man nodded and lifted a flap in the counter. He dropped his cigarette as he crossed to a door at the back. He went through the door and slammed it behind him. The dark man stepped on the glowing butt, grinding it into the floor as though it was an insect he very badly wanted to kill.

The man called Sid made several calls after he had finished his conversation with the boss. He arranged to meet three men immediately in a caff near Waterloo station.

One of the men he met in the caff had a hoarse voice and a running nose. One was young, with greasy shoulder-length hair. One was fat and wore a beard. Sid spoke for a few minutes, low-voiced.

When he had finished, two of his listeners nodded. The bearded man said, 'I can't get to bleedin' Dorset tonight, Sid. My old woman's havin' our fourth, see? Just took her into the hospital.'

'You can't have heard me right, Sammy,' said Sid. 'Silver Birch sent. Remember what he done to Micky the Peep when Micky wouldn't lend him a car?'

'I never heard the truth o' that,' said the greasy-haired youth. 'What did happen?'

'Silver cut his balls off an' handed them to Micky's kid daughter, wrapped up in a bit o' newspaper like fish an' chips. He was in one of his rages, see, 'cos Micky didn't do what he asked.'

'Remember what he done to his own missus, after she blew?' said the hoarse man, sniffing and wiping his nose on his sleeve. 'I had to watch that, but I sooner never. I never ha' believed one little razor blade could make such a mess of a face. The fuzz tried to make her say who done it, but o' course she never. She didn't dare. She couldn't talk, of course, not havin' no tongue no more, but she wrote down she didn't know who done it.'

'Well, he had a kind o' right,' said Sid. 'His own missus blowin', leavin' two kids. Definitely dodgy. Naturally put him in one of his rages. 'Sfunny, that cheery manner Silver has, shaking hands, buying rounds, an' all the time . . .'

''Sbeing single-minded,' said the hoarse man. 'That's what got him where he is. When he wants something nothing don't stand in his way. Won't accept no for an answer, Silver won't. If a bloke tells him no, Silver's all the more determined. 'Member when he set his heart on that betting shop in Stoke Newington? Bloke didn't want to sell. Silver was ever so smooth and friendly, till he got the message the bloke *wouldn't* sell. Then he saw red, like. He wanted that particular shop more'n any in London, just 'cos the bloke said no.'

'Did he get it?' asked the youth.

'What a bloody silly question,' said Sid. 'They never did find the bloke. Not surprising. He's pushing up sweet little primroses, in a deep hole in Epping Forest.'

Dan was up at dawn, picking mushrooms among the cattle in the watermeadows near the village. It was the best place for them — well grazed, well mucked. To get a good haul he had to be up before the rest of the world was awake, and before the cattle had trodden all over the crop. It amazed him, every year, the way a field bare in the evening was dotted with succulent white golf-balls in the morning. It was lucky no nocturnal animal liked mushrooms, except himself. If he fried them with a bit of bacon, he thought, his mother might fancy them.

She might fancy a bit of sloe gin, too, and blackberries and hazelnuts and rose-hip syrup. It was all there for the taking in the hedgerows. You had to look sharp to get hazelnuts, or the squirrels had them all. The blackberries were ripening in a most uneven way. You saw flowers and fruit on the same bit of bramble-bush, and some of the fruit tiny and green and just beginning to form, some red but still as hard as a stone, some black and juicy and ready to fall.

The robins were going 'chip-chip', as they did in the autumn, and the titmice were going 'see-saw' as though they thought it was spring. A lot of birds were still hiding. They'd moulted and they were still waiting for their winter plumage. Maybe they were cold, these mist-saturated mornings; maybe they felt ridiculous, looking half-plucked.

Wheeling his bicycle, picking occasional ripe blackberries, Dan passed a five-barred gate into a field. A tawny owl was sitting on the top bar. He was facing Dan, motionless as a heron. His face was a grey circle, flat as a plate, with a yellow beak and bright dark-brown eyes. He stared at Dan unwinking. He looked not so much wise as superior. Suddenly he turned round. He twisted his body, then shifted his feet, so that his back was to Dan. The plumage was very pretty, a warm reddy-brown with darker mottlings. Dan was puzzled. Did his own appearance disgust the bird? Did the bird think that by turning his back he had become invisible? Then the owl twisted his head round, right the way round so that he was looking exactly backwards. It was an impossible, a ridiculous position. He stared at Dan with those bright, unblinking, haughty, dark-brown eyes each side of the cruel yellow beak. Dan stared back, having some pride about being outfaced by a bird. At last the owl turned to his own front again, and flew unhurriedly away.

Dan was superstitious about some things. He was superstitious about being stared at by a back-to-front owl. He thought it was either a good omen or a bad omen. He had no idea which. Considering the mess he was in, he thought a bad omen was more likely.

He had his usual nap between breakfasts, while men in neat dark suits were hurrying into offices.

He bicycled to Sir George Simpson's to tidy the garden and make a bonfire. The bonfire was difficult to start as everything had been saturated by the heavy September dew. Once it started, the smoke rose like a solid white column in the still air. It was Dan's favourite smell, after lilies of the valley and roast pheasant.

Going to the Chestnut Horse for a pint at lunchtime, he saw a silver BMW parked by the pub. The smashed headlight had been replaced, but there was still a dent in the wing where the chestnut pony had kicked it.

They were back, then.

They were back, and drinking gin and tonic in the Chestnut Horse — not the fat spoiled child, but the parents. The child, it seemed, was distraught about losing the pony. They'd offered a reward, advertised in the *Horse and Hound*. They were offering a reward locally, too. The police had compiled a list of grey ponies, including several in a big dealer's yard, and some a party of Gipsies had. The Coxes had come down to try and identify theirs. They had inspected a lot of ponies, but not their pony. They were taking all this trouble on the child's account.

All this was broadcast in the bar of the Chestnut Horse. The reward was £100. A dozen pairs of ears pricked up. A dozen pairs of eyes would instantly be peeled, all the time, for the missing pony. When the reward was generally known, hundreds of eyes would be looking.

The police were looking hard.

Dan returned to his bonfire, wishing he could burn grey ponies in it. He found Lady Simpson prodding the fire. She said she had to go to Albany Farm.

'I tried to ring up Miss Hadfield,' she said, 'but their telephone is out of order. Most thoughtless of them. I want them to lend us a pony for the Michaelmas Fair. It is for charity, of course, so I hope I shall persuade them.'

Dan remembered the odd jobs the Morrisons wanted done. He said he would go to Albany too. Lady Simpson, as he expected, offered him a lift.

'Thankee, ma'am, thankee kindlee,' said Dan, giving her his broadest pixie grin and torturing his cap in his hands.

In the car, he promised to give his help at the Michaelmas Fair, which was in aid of the County Association of Youth Clubs. Dan had only a dim idea of what went on at youth clubs — no kind of club had played any part in his life — but he pledged his support. He had a moment of nightmare, imagining the Hadfield sisters lending the Surrey grey pony for the Fair. It was highly unlikely. They were unlikely to lend any pony. Clubs had played no part in their lives either; and what they wanted youth to do was come and have riding lessons.

They got to the little blind turning of the farm lane which led to Albany. It was blocked. Three big trees had been felled across it. Beyond the trees, twenty yards away, the lane was further blocked by a caravan.

A man came out of the caravan carrying a power saw. He was a big, powerful man, built much on the lines of Eddie Birch, but swarthy instead of fair and about Dan's age. Dan expected him to begin cutting up the felled trees, but instead he started on the trunk of a fourth tree.

'Why?' said Lady Simpson, shocked. 'Those were splendid trees. I've often admired them.'

'New tenant o' the land,' said the man with the saw. He had a London voice, a Cockney voice. 'Reckons them trees is dangerous.'

He said he did not know who the new tenant was. He and his mates had orders from their own gaffer.

Dan thought he knew who the new tenant was.

'I wonder why they've come in a caravan?' mused Lady Simpson. 'They surely don't expect to be here for days and days, do they?'

Dan thought he knew the answer to that one, too.

'I suppose they're elms,' said Lady Simpson vaguely. 'I suppose they've got the blight. What a shame.'

'Sorry about this,' said the man with the saw. 'You can walk up to the farm, though. 'Snot far.'

It was too far for Lady Simpson in her smart shoes. She told Dan she would wait until the Hadfields' telephone was mended, or the tree-trunks were sawn up and cleared away. The Michaelmas Fair was not until the 29th. There was time enough to make the arrangements.

Dan climbed over the felled trees. The lane was choked with healthy leaves just beginning to turn, on springy twigs and spreading branches. The whole thing made an immense barrier which was awkward even for Dan to climb over. It would have been awkward to go round, too. There were high banks crowned with a jungle of brambles. A bigger detour would have taken him into a sea of brambles, some shoulder-high, some twice a man's height. The scraggy, useless woodland had been waste ground for years, for the whole of Dan's lifetime. Dan could cross it if he had to, but he didn't want to — his clothes and his skin tore as easily as anybody else's.

There was no question of Lady Simpson climbing in, even if she wanted to walk to the farm. There was no question of the Hadfield sisters climbing out.

There was no sign of blight in the felled trees. They were oaks.

The door of the caravan was open. Two men were inside, drinking beer out of cans. One was large and fat, with a beard; he looked like a professional wrestler. The other was much younger, with greasy shoulder-length hair. They were sharply dressed for tree-fellers.

Dan greeted them politely, in his broadest Wessex. The bearded man nodded. The youth lit a cigarette. Neither said anything.

Dan walked to the farm, seeing nobody, and on to the cottage. He wondered what the Morrisons made of the blocked drive. The curtains were drawn over all the cottage windows. Dan rang the new bell, which bonged electronically on the other side of the door. The door was locked. There was no sign of the Morrisons' car.

It was thoughtless of them to ask him to come, and then to be away when he came.

He turned and trudged away, back towards the farm. As he neared the Morrisons' boundary he glanced back at the cottage. An upstairs curtain twitched. Dan thought it had been drawn back a little so that someone could see out. It had been pulled back into place as he turned. He was sure there was someone in the cottage. But there was no car, no smoke, no sign of life except the brief movement of one curtain.

Dan wondered if the Morrisons were being burgled. He doubted it. He had inspected the contents of the cottage, and only the record-player tempted him. There was nothing to interest Miss Huxtable at 'The Box of Delights'. The electrical gadgets in the kitchen were expensive, but a thief would need a car. The mixer and liquidizer and eye-level grill were heavy. A thief would need a car for anything bigger than the spoons, and the spoons were not worth taking.

A squatter was unlikely, with the Morrisons presumably due back. Except, of course, that they couldn't get back, not in their car, not until the trees were cleared.

Dan wondered how the person in the cottage had got in. The Morrisons had taken a lot of trouble, because the place was empty so much of the time. The new casement windows had metal frames and burglar-proof catches. The new door had a Chubb double-turn lock. You'd have to break something. Nothing was broken.

Someone lurking in the cottage fitted in with healthy oak trees being felled across the lane.

Dan walked slowly to the farmhouse. Rounding the corner of the stables, he stepped over the shallow pit he had recently dug to take a new water butt. There were two hedgehogs in the pit, unable to climb out. Dan wondered what had attracted them there. They ate slugs, snails, worms, mice; Dan's father had said they ate snakes and lizards too, and even rats, but Dan had never seen them doing so. Probably these ones were on their way to a dry ditch under a hedge, where they would make a nest for their winter sleep. One had scraped himself a little trench in the bottom of the pit; he lay there, half rolled up, jumping nervously when Dan moved or made a noise, his spines up-ended for defence. Dan rescued him, careful of the sharp spines. The other one was dead. Dan picked it up. Even in his own preoccupation, he was sorry for the dead hedgehog and for the lonely survivor. He took the dead one into the tackroom, with a vague idea that the spines ought to be useful for something, such as fishing-floats or weapons or tools.

Miss Hettie was in the tackroom, rubbing stirrup leathers with saddle soap. Dan asked her about the Morrisons. He was astonished at the bitterness of Miss Hettie's outburst.

'Someone's there now,' said Dan, the sharpness of his disquiet making him use, as he never used to the nobs, his normal educated voice.

'Possibly,' said Miss Hettie. 'Probably. A car came by here last night, quite late, when we were on our way to bed. I suppose it was that jumped-up lout from London. The car went away again soon afterwards. I suppose he dropped someone, or someone drove the car away for him.'

'Oh,' said Dan. 'Then they had those trees down this morning.'

'What trees, boy? What are you talking about?'

Dan told her about the trees, the caravan, and the unnamed new tenant of Fred Mortimer's executors.

Miss Hettie called indoors to her sister, then strode down the drive to investigate the outrage. Dan followed her, unnerving theories flooding into his mind.

The fourth tree was down across the lane.

'What is the meaning of this?' cried Miss Hettie imperiously to the swarthy man with the power saw. 'What is your authority for this? How am I to get my car out? I have a right of way here. These trees must be removed at once.'

'They will be, lady, soon's we can,' said the swarthy man, politely enough.

'When?'

'Ah. There's loads to come down.'

'By whose orders?'

'I dunno, lady. We're doin' what we're paid for. Now 'scuse me, please, I got to get on.'

He restarted his saw. It snarled deafeningly, like a small unsilenced motorbike. Miss Hettie screamed against the noise, but the man shrugged apologetically and attacked a fifth tree, a tall ash.

Miss Hettie drew Dan up the lane, where she could talk over the noise of the saw.

'I know who's behind this,' she said.

Dan nodded.

'But he won't budge us.'

Dan shook his head.

"If they don't clear the lane we'll get the police.'

'How?' asked Dan.

Miss Hettie looked at him with pitying contempt. In her eyes, he knew, he was of no value as an ally. He was only good mending fences and helping at gymkhanas. She turned and strode back towards the farm. Every stride she took expressed an arrogant determination to hold what she had.

Dan looked at the car hitched to the caravan. It was a Triumph 2000, dirty, not new. He memorized the number on the off-chance it might be useful.

Beyond the huge screen of the felled trees he saw the roof of another vehicle. It stopped at the mouth of the lane. Dan could hear nothing over the noise of the power saw. He saw the vehicle back and turn.

Dan climbed the felled trees. The bearded man was out in the road. He had been talking, no doubt, to the driver of the vehicle.

The vehicle was well away by the time Dan was over the trees. It was a small yellow van. It was a Post Office van. It was a telephone engineer. He had been sent away.

6

Dan thought: it can't go on. Not nowadays. Not in the calm south-west of England. The Post Office telephone engineer would be back — he must be. The postman, the milkman, the feed-merchant, the grocer. The men can't keep the lane blocked. Somebody must go and complain to the police, in a day or less than a day. The trees would have to be moved. In a day, or less than a day, the Hadfields would be able to drive in and out. Their telephone would be mended, too.

Would the police go to Albany Farm itself? Search? See the grey pony from Surrey? Ask Miss Trixie where she got it?

And then ask among the Milchester antique dealers, and prod about in the back premises of 'The Box of Delights'? And get an innocent description from Miss Huxtable of the seller of eight antique clocks?

Dan decided that he needed to know more. He bicycled into Medwell village, changed some silver for a pocketful of coppers, and waited to use the public telephone-box.

He waited for twenty minutes for the telephone. Then he rang the Milchester exchange; he reported (as a dozen people must have done; as Lady Simpson had done) that the Albany Farm telephone was out of order.

'Just a moment,' said a girl's cool voice. After a long moment of buzzes and clicks, the voice told Dan that the telephone had been disconnected at the request of the subscriber.

The girl could tell Dan no more.

He pondered for a minute, surrendering the telephone-box to young Harry Barnett the water-keeper, whose name he borrowed for his dealings with 'The Box of Delights'.

A letter, probably typed and with some kind of scrawled signature, had gone to the Telephone Manager in Milchester. Probably delivered by hand, the minute the first tree was down, at a pre-arranged moment. Or the request had been made by telephone, by someone speaking for Miss Trixie Hadfield or her sister, asking for the telephone to be cut off because it kept them awake, or they couldn't afford it, or they no longer needed it.

They needed it terribly.

The engineer had not come to mend the telephone. He had come to take it away. There was no hurry about that. The Post Office could wait for days, or even for weeks, before removing an unwanted telephone.

Dan thought he had better confirm what was already a normal certainty. He knew Fred Mortimer had made a will, which involved appointing an executor. Dan knew about wills and executors from his hated days at the Bank. He had worked for a time — a time of especial grief — in the Trustee Department of the Bank. It was highly likely that Fred's executor was a local solicitor. That would be a normal and sensible choice — a reliable professional man who knew Fred, knew his affairs (the legal ones), and knew the oafish sons Fred had left his fortune to. Dan had no idea which solicitors, which firm.

Dan borrowed the classified directory from Bert Monger in the village shop, which was also the sub-Post Office. He looked through the yellow pages. There were a great many solicitors in Milchester, a surprising number, and many more in Ighampton and other nearby towns.

Dan began telephoning, in a clipped bank manager's voice. He worked his way through the alphabet. Some of the calls were brief, when small offices had intelligent girls on the switchboard; some were long, as partner after partner was sleepily consulted. Most of the lawyers knew Fred Mortimer's name, owing to the sensational manner of his recent death; a few had had dealings with him when they acted for the vendors of land Fred bought. When he reached the letter S, Dan was beginning to despair. But the firm of Tanner, Oliphant and Burton was the right one.

Dan spoke to Mr Oliphant — banker to lawyer — and said he was interested in the purchase of sixty acres of the late Mr Mortimer's estate, a tract which had once formed part of Albany Farm.

'I'm afraid you're too late, Mr Huxtable,' said Mr Oliphant. 'I know the piece of mixed woodland to which you refer. By an extraordinary coincidence an option to purchase has already been granted, just yesterday granted, together with a terminable tenancy pending exchange of contracts.'

'May I know the identity of the tenant?' asked Dan, in his most glib and deferential banker's voice. 'I do not, of course, ask you to betray a confidence, but I contemplate making a direct approach to him.'

'There is, as it happens, no confidentiality here at all, sir. The tenant and prospective purchaser is rather anxious than otherwise that his identity and intention should be generally known. He even discussed with us inserting a notice in the *Milchester Argus,* but we persuaded him that, pending finalization, this would be premature.'

'Oh,' said Dan, much surprised.

'His family farmed the property for many generations, and he is most anxious to regain it himself and to bring up his own children there. I myself do not remember his father, but my own father does. Though I naturally sympathize with you, Mr Huxtable, in your disappointment, I am bound to admit a still keener sympathy with Mr Birch's plan and with his sense of family tradition. Refreshing in these times, is it not? It is difficult to fail to find it refreshing. Quite apart from that, as executor of the late Mr Mortimer's estate I am obliged to negotiate terms as favourable as possible, on behalf of the legatees, and Mr Birch's terms are *very* favourable.'

'I daresay I couldn't match them,' said Dan.

'Perhaps you could, sir, but I daresay you might not wish to. Mr Birch values the land above its market price, frankly, because of his family's association with it. Here again, I am betraying no confidence. The figures will be published. Incidentally, Mr Birch had already made a successful offer for the remainder of Albany Farm, and for the farmhouse itself, his family's old home.'

'He can't have,' said Dan.

"I assure you. He told me so himself. He is already in touch with solicitors acting for the present owners. A London firm. I do not know the name. That is not a negotiation in which we have any standing. Of course contracts have not been exchanged, but an offer has been made and accepted.'

Dan hung up, deeply puzzled. Mr Oliphant the executor was

quite certain he had his facts right. He had been encouraged to broadcast them, to put about the good news that the Birch family were back in Albany after half a century. His source was Eddie Birch, whom he naturally believed.

Eddie Birch was making no secret of his attempts to get Albany back, all of it. He was declaring that he was responsible for having the trees down, for blocking the Hadfields' right of way, for sending away the telephone engineer.

He was declaring that the Hadfields had accepted his offer. How *could* he do that, if they hadn't? They had only to say different. Local people would soon know different. Eddie Birch's bluff would be called in a moment — in a day or less than a day.

What he was trying was blankly impossible. This was obvious. It must be as obvious to Eddie Birch as to Dan.

Therefore, it wasn't a bluff. It couldn't be. Something had happened at Albany since Dan was there, something to justify Eddie Birch talking to the Hadfields' London lawyer. A still bigger offer? A threat? A combination of the two?

But the Hadfields weren't interested in any offer Eddie Birch could make. Threats would only make them more obstinate. Miss Hettie was quite capable of loosing off with the old 16-bore if the threats got open and vicious. And if they didn't, they wouldn't work.

What could have happened at Albany, in that short time, to make the obstinate old ladies change their minds? If something weird had happened, would it eventually bring the police out there? Would they see and identify the extra grey pony, and find out how it got there?

Dan went thoughtfully to the Chestnut Horse.

Bert Monger was there — he always looked in when he had put up the shutters of the General Stores.

'Ah,' said Bert to Ted Goldingham the landlord, when Dan came into the pub. 'He'll know, Dan Mallett will, seein' he goes there constant.'

'Eh?' said Dan. He pitched his voice at its Chestnut Horse level, about midway between bank manager and treacly yokel.

'Those old ladies. Those Misses Hadfield.'

'What about 'em?'

'They suddenly ben an' sold out. That Eddie Birch, he told me himself. Cam' into the shop an hour back, when I was gettin' ready to shut. Says who 'e was. "Gum," I says, "anythin' to do wi' old Will Birch at Albany?" "That I am,' he says. "I come a tidy way," he says, "since my Dad were levered out o' the farm by a rich bastard wi' a clever lawyer. But I got un back," he says, "same like I always dreamed I would. Matter o' fact," he says, "the old ladies was glad enough to sell. They're too old to manage that place," he says, "an' I believe the doctor said so. They was hangin' on till the end o' the school holidays," he says, "so as not to disappoint the nippers. Now they gone to a relative. Somebody's given 'em a home. I reckon they'll be missed hereabouts," he says, "but I'll try an' fill the gap. I bought the ridin' school an' the ponies, the whole boilin','" he says, "I'm not capable o' runnin' that lot,' he says, "but I got a girl who knows un inside out, a trained groom like, an she can teach me. An' teach my kids," he says, "an' everybody else's kids. Business as usual," he says, "under new management." So he gives me an order for groceries, to be dropped at the end of the drive. And he gives me the address for forwardin' the old ladies' post.'

'Where?' asked Dan.

'Midlands. Bedfordshire or summat.'

'They actually ben and gone?' asked Dan, incredulous.

'Seems so. Yer, they must've.'

'Sounds like good news,' said Ted Goldingham on the other side of the bar. "Will Birch was afore my time, but my old man knew him. He didn't hardly come in here, 'cause he couldn't afford a drink. But I su'pose the son might come in. Hear about his car? He can afford a drink all night. I never saw the old ladies here. Too high an' mighty for pubs. No loss to me. No loss to the village, the way they looked down their noses at folks. It's nice to think o' the farm goin' back to the Birches.'

'And Eddie Birch's kids bein' brought up there,' agreed Bert Monger. 'An' the ponies looked after an' all.'

Dan finished his pint and bicycled homewards, wondering if it was too soon to give his mother roast pheasant again. Her diet had to be varied, or she got bored with her food and ate even less than usual.

He wondered very hard what had happened at Albany.

If Eddie Birch was in legal possession of the whole original farm, then the lane was his lane, the right of way his right of way. The trees could stay there as long as he liked. Things could be delivered at the mouth of the land — food, milk, feed for the ponies. He could bring his dustbins to the mouth of the lane, for the cart that came by on Thursdays. The only person inconvenienced was himself.

No — that was wrong. If he was legally there, he had won. He'd have the trees away in the morning.

No — that was still wrong. The trees must be away already, or the Hadfields couldn't have left.

Could they have left, so quickly? Packed it all up? Furniture, pictures, books, all the oddments of fifty years' residence?

Well, they'd let Albany furnished, then — left everything behind for the time being, and gone off to the relatives in Bedfordshire.

It was impossible that they should have left so quickly. For that matter, it was impossible that several big trees could have been cleared from the lane so quickly.

Dan went the long way round, by Yewstop and then Albany, although his dogs, pigeons, bantams and mother would all be impatient for their supper.

He wondered if the girl groom was there, the one he had very much liked the look of. She'd been grand when the fat spoiled Surrey child screamed at Birch's little girl. She'd enlisted under Birch. She was going to run the riding school. She was running the stables already.

She knew the grey pony. She'd looked after it for months. She'd recognize it instantly.

Feeling a little sick, Dan bicycled past the Albany lane.

The trees were still there. Beyond them, blocking the lane, was the caravan.

The thing to do was to go to the police. The last thing Dan could possibly do was to go to the police.

Dan bicycled slowly on, inspecting Eddie Birch's new estate without seeming to do so.

He saw that the undergrowth near the road had been trampled, and here and there cut back with a hook. He saw the reason. A new, five-strand barbed-wire fence had been put up, in the trees a little back from the road. Few posts had been used. The wire had been stapled to the trunks. It was a formidable fence, the strands close together, the top high, the whole almost hidden by brambles and bracken. By day it could be watched. By night it was a hell of an obstacle.

Someone had been working hard and fast. A five-strand fence, threading heavy undergrowth, was a lot of labour. But it had been put up since Dan left the farm. That must be beyond the three men of the caravan. Eddie Birch had brought in more men. An army of men from London? He had collected them off a train, maybe, or from their own cars left in Milchester. He had ferried them here in his Mercedes. Now they were camped, or sharing the caravan. Or perhaps, the job done, they'd gone back to London again?

The river-mist rose clammily from the cold bottom ground. The haws spangled the hedges like drops of a rainstorm of blood. Dan passed a patch of hedge over which woody-nightshade berries were strung like beads of coral, and another full of the fruit of the white briony. Guelder-rose leaves were turning scarlet and dogwood leaves purple. The fat clusters of elderberries were already ripe, black and shiny as miniature currants. A few birds were singing, after weeks or months of silence. The breeding pairs had almost all broken up and the winter parties were assembling. As he bicycled slowly home, Dan found that he was keeping pace with an army, prettier than Eddie Birch's army. The vanguard was a flock of long-tailed titmice, peeping constantly to each other as though afraid of losing touch. After them came a small party of tree-creepers, with silver tummies and querulous squeaky voices; then some marsh-titmice, with their black caps always falling forward over their eyes and their cry of 'chew-chew', as though they were telling each other to eat up before the weather got colder.

Dan watched them all absently as he pedalled, reading the signs and reading behind the signs. When the little birds gathered into these sociable groups, all living creatures were adjusting to the coming of winter, changing their habits or habitats. Pheasants, partridges, woodcocks, hares and rabbits and roedeer — they ate different things because there were different things to eat. Dan, who lived on these creatures and among them, had to change his methods accordingly.

A loop of the river, mist-shrouded, put him in mind of something else. When the titmice gathered, it was time to stop poaching hen brown trout from the river. They were getting thin and flaccid and full of roe. Some of the young cock fish would be all right for a while, but a plump grayling was best at this time of year, coming to the pink of its condition because it spawned at a different season. Nature, thought Dan, was very considerate. When one thing went off the menu, something else replaced it. His mother fancied a young grayling, scaled and split and fried with a bit of bacon.

In an office, Dan remembered with a shudder, one season was like another. When it got cold, they switched on the central heating. All the problems were the same, all the challenges. It was as dull in October as in April. Dan's problems were constantly different, changing with the year, endlessly fascinating. Each new thing he learned showed a new door to something still to be learned. There was nothing Dan envied about anybody else's life.

But his own life left a bit to be desired at the moment. He turned his mind from birds and berries to examine his own intentions.

He was frightened for the Hadfields. They were terrible old women in a lot of ways, but he respected their guts and their consistency. He had known them all his life. They looked after their ponies as Dan looked after his own animals.

Was that the lever Eddie Birch had used? A threat to the ponies? That might shift the Hadfields as no threat to themselves would do. But Eddie Birch wanted the ponies. He had already, he said, bought the ponies.

All kinds of ideas rushed through Dan's mind, of weapons Eddie Birch might have used against the Hadfields. Some of the ideas were sickening.

Were the Hadfields still inside, beyond the blocked lane, rimmed by barbed wire?

If the trees and the caravan and the wire were keeping the Hadfields in, they were also keeping the rest of the world out. Legally, if what Eddie Birch said was true. A man was allowed to wire his own land and block his own driveway.

The irony lay in the Hadfields' own reputation. Bert Monger and Ted Goldingham had accepted without surprise that the crusty old ladies had left suddenly, without saying good-bye to anybody. It fitted with the Hadfields as they knew them — a law unto themselves, eccentric, rude, high-handed, apt to behave in a way unaccountable to ordinary people, to the Mongers and Goldinghams of the world.

It *was* in character that the sisters might suddenly up sticks and go. If they decided to go, they might easily do it just as Bert Monger had reported they had done it. They wouldn't be interested in farewells. They were not on close terms with anybody. They despised nearly everybody. Dan doubted if they ever went into the houses of other nobs; he was sure other nobs never went into their house. They couldn't be bothered with human beings, except as tradesmen or servants or paying pupils. Their relationships were with horses. They'd say good-bye to them, but not to Bert Monger or Lady Simpson . . .

Say good-bye to all their ponies? Suddenly, like that? Never. It was not to be believed.

Among the ponies at Albany — which Eddie Birch might or might not have bought, which he might or might not have mutilated — was the grey pony from Surrey. Known to the girl groom.

Dan's intentions were suddenly clear. The pony tipped the scale, tipped it extremely heavily. Dan had to get to Albany, at once, tonight. There were lots of reasons. He was full of curiosity to know what had happened to the Hadfields. He was concerned about them. But, above all, he had to remove that pony. When that was safely done, he could get the police in, if it seemed desirable.

'From what you say about those trees,' said Miss Trixie Hadfield to her sister, 'we can't get out.'

'Not for the moment. The man was quite civil. I don't suppose it will be long.'

'At the same time, no one can get in.'

'Not without a helicopter.'

'What an absurd remark. None of our pupils have such things, or the tradesmen either.'

It's an ill wind, Miss Trixie thought. Inconvenient though the blocked drive might be, it enabled her to do one creature a good turn. Feeling it safe to do so, she took the new grey pony out into a paddock with others. As a precaution, probably quite needless, she put it in the paddock furthest from the outside world, the one bordered by the post-and-rail of the cowman's cottage.

Libby Franklin was bored.

She understood that she was taking care of the cottage for Mr Birch; she was making a base for him, on his land, where he could telephone and rest and have a meal. She saw the need for this, and she was glad to help, since the promise of the future was so bright. But there were no books in the cottage, no records or record-player, no radio, nothing. The previous owners had taken all those things away. There were not even any pictures on the walls to look at. The place was perfectly comfortable, but there was nothing whatever to do.

Libby had promised Mr Birch to stay close inside the cottage so as not to spark off a row. The sight of her face was enough to enrage the ridiculous old women, after what had happened. Mr Birch said he still wanted to do it pleasant and friendly, to get them to change their minds and sign a document saying so. This was so obviously right that Libby obeyed his orders.

She telephoned her mother and one or two friends. She did not want to run up too much of a bill, precisely because Mr Birch had been so generous. The only other diversion she allowed herself was an occasional peep out of the upstairs window. She had seen the attractive brown-faced man with the astonishing blue eyes. He had come and gone. He was an enemy: he was on the side of the old women. It was a great pity. Libby found she was intrigued by some quality the man had. He was not quite like anybody she had ever met. He was somehow a chameleon, but without pretence. Stumping about in his gaiters at the gymkhana, he was the most complete yokel, a caricature of a yokel. But face to face, talking in a gentle educated voice, he was a million miles from being a yokel — less a yokel than Mr Cox, less even than Mr Birch. Perhaps there were other such men in Dorset, but there were certainly none in Surrey.

When he came across the garden, part of her wanted to open the cottage door and ask him in to tea. But she kept quiet and waited for him to disappear.

Far away, among trees, she saw workmen busy about something.

Early in the evening she peeped again, and saw the older of the old women leading a grey pony towards the cottage. She put the pony in the paddock nearest the cottage. It looked completely different from the other ponies there, in conformation and movement and quality. It looked like a thoroughbred in a parcel of cabhorses.

With an incredulous shock, Libby recognized the pony.

She could not imagine the Coxes selling Hector. She could not imagine Melissa letting them do so. She could not imagine the old women finding the stiff price the Coxes would ask — and rightly — if they did sell. They couldn't afford such a pony; it was out of their class.

Obviously they had stolen it, or bought it from a thief.

Libby reached for the telephone to call the police.

She paused, her hand a foot above the telephone. She had never dialled 999 for emergency services, and did not want to make a fool of herself the first time she did so. The old sisters *might* have bought the pony. Or it *might* be Hector's twin. If the police came and looked at the pony, and it was the Hadfields' pony, Libby would look an absolute nit. Worse, she would look a nit with a grudge, trying to get her own back by giving the police false information. The old bags would be furious, and this time they'd have a right to be. The atmosphere would be even sourer than before, which was exactly what Mr Birch didn't want.

There was another aspect. If the pony was Hector, then he was here instead of at the Coxes'. He was free from Melissa's whip and weight and hands and ill-temper. Hector, if it was Hector, was better away from Melissa.

It was Hector all right. The longer Libby looked at the pony, through the crack in the curtain, the more sure she was. The old woman receded, stumping in her boots back towards the farmhouse. Libby remembered her rage and humiliation, and her hand descended towards the telephone. If the pony had been stolen, the Coxes would have reported it. Advertised. Offered a reward. The police would be looking for it. They would be glad to be told about the pony Libby could see, even if the pony wasn't Hector. It would be lovely to see the old women dragged into court as receivers of stolen goods.

Libby's hand paused again, inches from the telephone. She was completely undecided.

As he expected to be riding a pony home, Dan walked to Albany, setting off soon after midnight. He had had a full day, but he had had a good sleep, too, after his mother was tucked up.

He wore a leather jacket which made him look like a tearaway on a motorcycle (and had once belonged to such a person); it was black, which was good, and it might stand an onslaught of thorns better than a tweed coat or a woolly sweater. In his pockets were the flask of whisky, the clasp-knife and the pencil flashlight which he always took with him at night. In his hand was the home-made blackthorn stick with the lump of lead in the knob, which he always took. He also had a pair of heavy pliers, up to cutting wire, and a small billhook, up to slashing brambles. He felt overburdened for a long walk, but it was the lesser evil.

Life at the moment seemed to Dan a matter of choosing between evils.

He thought of getting to Albany by water, crossing the river where it looped round the old crowman's cottage. There were serious snags. It meant rowing a long way upstream from the village, where the only boats were. They were Dr Smith's boats, kept in a locked shed. No other boats were allowed, because of the fishing. The boat would have to stay behind after Dan landed, to be found by Eddie Birch's men. Or it would drift downstream and be lost for ever. That would be hard on Dr Smith, which influenced Dan, though not overwhelmingly.

Swimming might have served. Dan wished he had learned. His education, so rich in some directions, was thin in others. But the pony could swim. All animals could, as far as Dan knew — certainly all horses. Whether it would go into cold running water, in the dark, in a strange place, was another question. If it did, the problem of getting it away from Albany disappeared. Dan would not try to ride it in the water, but he could hold on, and steer it downstream to any of a dozen feasible landing places.

He gulped at the thought of holding on to the pony's mane, in the deep waters of the river, in pitch darkness. But it was better than going to prison for stealing the pony and the clocks, which was clearly the alternative.

Another choice of evils.

After Yewstop and the river woods, Dan prowled delicately to the boundary of Albany Farm, to the piece which Fred Mortimer had bought and Eddie Birch now occupied.

Occupied was right, like a conquered country — ringed with barbed-wire, probably patrolled. Dan wondered about dogs, electric fences, trip-wires, gin-traps.

With the weighted blackthorn in his right hand, and the billhook in his left, and the big pliers heavy in his hip pocket, he crept up to the new five-strand fence. If the pony wouldn't swim, he must come out this way. He snipped the bottom strand close to the trunk of the birch it was stapled to. The wire pinged when it was cut, and lashed away to the right. Dan tucked the loose end safely into a bank of brambles. The leaves felt clammy in the mist, and the ground squelched. The thorns were no less sharp for being wet. Tendrils of the brambles grabbed at Dan's arms and ankles in the dark, as dangerous as the springy coils of barbed wire.

Dan cut the second strand, and the third. As he cut the third he felt a jolt of electricity. It was not a severe shock. Far away to his left, muffled by the river mist, an electric bell jangled. He thought it was at the mouth of the farm lane to Albany. The caravan was there. Men were there. Dan froze, crouching, listening. In the stillness of the night he heard a car's engine start. He thought there were two cars. He saw the glow of headlights on the road. They had cars on the road, outside the barrier of the trees across the lane.

Eddie Birch was doing nothing illegal. He was simply guarding his property. Thousands of building contractors, warehousemen, factory owners did the same thing, using the same methods.

The glow approached as one of the cars crept along the little road beside the boundary fence. There was too much light. It was pointing in the wrong direction. There was a searchlight mounted on the car, as well as the headlights. The searchlight was swivelled at right-angles to the car's axis; it was sweeping and probing the fence at the edge of the woods.

Dan slid under the two uncut strands of barbed wire, into the wood, away from the raking implacable searchlight and the men's shouts. Immediately he was waist-deep in brambles, which clutched at him and tore at his ankles and trousers. It was almost impossible to get through the entanglement of brambles. A blink of light from his flash showed a sea of them ahead, an ocean of hostile tendrils, strong as wire, dense as a carpet, waist and shoulder and head high, armed with billions of long thorns.

The car was nearer, and the searchlight.

7

Dan could not go forwards or sideways, owing to the towering en-
tanglements of brambles. He could slash a way through them with
his billhook, the noise of the car and the dog hiding his efforts: but
not in time. He could not go upwards — there was no climbable
tree within reach. He could not go backwards without walking into
the oncoming beam of the searchlight.

He could only go downwards. Unpleasant as it was, down he
went, burrowing into the intensely hostile vegetation, grabbed, lacerated. He was by no means sure he was invisible, if the beam of
the searchlight probed in the right direction. The brambles were
low behind him, by the fence. The bracken and tall grass of the
verge had been trampled. Would the bright new barbed-wire be
continuously visible in the beam of the searchlight, or was much of
it hidden by branches and undergrowth? Would the three missing
strands be seen?

Presumably they knew the wire had been cut. The bell told them
that. A circuit had been broken. But they would have no idea
where it was cut. At least, Dan thought not, but electricity was another of the subjects where his education was incomplete.

Where it was complete was in what he was doing now: avoiding
capture on someone else's property, curling up like a hedgehog, like
a field-mouse, quiet as a molehill, immobile as a tree-stump. Gamekeepers without number over the years had clumped their boots
down inches from his head without seeing him, although he lay
hard by the pheasants' creepways to set his snares.

The car stopped moving, although the engine was still running.
The searchlight probed backwards and forwards, up and down. It
must be mounted on a universal joint, Dan thought, instead of a
simple swivel. Eddie Birch was dauntingly well equipped. Suddenly, all the brambles round Dan were incandescent in a bath of

brilliant light. The beam mocked the river mist, at least at short distances. This distance was very short.

There was a hoarse shout. Dan heard the word 'wire'. Someone had spotted the gap in the fence, or an incompletely hidden loose end.

Dan had been careless. He had not thought of a thousand-watt searchlight mounted on a car. He was not used to having all this modern technology thrown against him. He cursed himself for a country mouse up against sharp big-city brains with all the ironmongery.

Heavy feet crashed towards the fence. They were very near Dan. Shadows of men flickered across the brilliantly lit nest of brambles where Dan lay huddled. They were interrupting the beam of their own searchlight: but not much, or for long.

'Gawd,' said a voice, a shrill voice with a London twang, 'look at that lot. No bastard couldn't get through that.'

'Somebody bin an' cut this wire,' said a hoarser voice, 'what I put here meself this afternoon. Bleedin' vandals. It'll have to be fixed first thing.'

'Fix it now,' said a voice Dan knew, a strong deep voice with only a trace of London accent.

'Have a heart, Silver.'

'Fix it now.'

'The bleeder bin an' cut the wire, an' then heard us, an' couldn't go on through them brambles, so he run away —'

'Yes. Fix the wire. Do it straight away. George, you stay and help. Come back to the lane when the fence is tight. I mean tight. I'll look at it in the morning. God help you if I'm not satisfied. Keep your ears open. If there's anyone hanging around, I want him. Any shape. I don't care what shape he's in. Any snooper, I want him. Got it?'

Grumbling, but softly, the hoarse-voiced man and the shrill-voiced man got tools and a lantern out of the car. They put the lantern on the ground by the fence, and began replacing the cut wires. Dan made no attempt to steal a glance at them, but since he knew what they were doing he could identify the various sounds they made with wire-cutters, pliers, staples, hammers.

The car's doors slammed. The car turned and went slowly away.

The glow of the electric lantern replaced the wild white glare of the searchlight. It was a strong enough light for the men to see Dan by, if they shone it in the right direction. But as long as it was on the ground, Dan was in deep shadow — a few inches of shadow, but enough.

Dan took no advantage of this. There was none he could take. Any movement among the brambles would make a noise like a bale of straw in a mincer. Even Dan, who could move as quietly as a grass-snake, could not budge without scrunching the brambles that girdled him. He had to wait till they went. Meanwhile he continued to imitate a hedgehog, a molehill, a cowpat, curled up tight to the ground, as still and silent as a stone. He was in agony. Brambles gouged at his cheeks. His mouth was full of wet leaf-mould. Tendrils of brambles had somehow coiled round his legs and his arms and his buttocks, as though he had been there for months; everywhere they bit into him with their vicious thorns. Cramp threatened his left thigh. There were insects down his back and one in his eye.

He was still choosing the lesser evil.

'There,' said the shrill voice with satisfaction. 'Good as new.'

The hoarse voice grunted.

With the corner of his eye, Dan saw the light swing upwards, as the lantern was picked up off the ground. Whoever held it swung it idly at the brambles beyond the fence. And then downwards. Dan felt himself bathed in light.

'What's that? Ol' clothes? By Christ, it's a man.'

Dan struggled to his feet. Brambles grabbed at his clothes and flesh. He heard cloth tearing, and felt long, savage lacerations on his legs and arms and face. There was still no way he could go. Behind him now, between him and the road, was the mended five-strand fence with the alarm in the third strand. He could climb it, but while climbing it he would be completely helpless. The beam of the lantern shone full at him. He could not hide his face. He could not see the two men, since they were behind the lantern. He wondered if they were armed. If so, arming them was Eddie Birch's single illegal act so far. His next, no doubt, would be what he did to Dan.

Dan wondered very hard, for a split second, what Eddie Birch

would do to him — and whether he had already done it, or something else, to the Hadfield sisters.

He felt the uncomfortable bulk of the heavy pliers in his hip
pocket. A perfect missile. The best possible. He pulled out the pliers.

There was a hoarse shout, unintelligible, from the other side of
the fence. The men thought he was pulling out a gun. He threw the
pliers full at the lantern, between the strands of wire. He hit the
lantern as hard as the shoe of the chestnut pony had hit the BMW's
headlight. There was a crash, a tinkle of glass, a wail of dismay,
sudden and total darkness.

'Get Silver,' said the shrill voice urgently. 'Quick. Lights an'
bangers. He can't get far, not in that jungle.'

'Yer,' said the hoarse voice. 'Right.'

One of the invisible figures blundered away. He fell heavily in
the sparse undergrowth between the fence and the verge, swore
passionately, and blundered in.

He'd be back very quick, with car and searchlight, with Eddie
Birch, with guns.

Dan's eyes rapidly grew used to the darkness after the glare of
the lantern. His night vision, he knew, was much better than most
people's, presumably because he used it so much more than most
people. The darkness was not absolute. Out of doors, darkness
never was. Dan could see the silhouette of the shrill-voiced man, a
blacker patch on the blackness. The man was close up against the
fence, standing rigid, listening.

'Now see here, friend,' said Dan in a high, whining voice that
completely disguised his own voice. 'We can come to an arrange-
ment, you an' me —'

'Piss off,' said the shrill man.

Dan's words and his wheedling tone had enabled him to move to
within a yard of the fence without alarming or alerting the man. It
was enough. He could not see the shrill man's head clearly, but he
saw where the head must be. He took his blackthorn stick by the
ferrule at the bottom, and swung it over the top of the fence at the
other's head. It hit with a magnificent clunk. There was a crash as
the man went down. There was a thin moan from the ground. The
man was not knocked out completely. But he was disabled, and

would stay so long enough for Dan to snip a strand of wire and snake under.

Snip with what? He had sacrificed his wire-cutters.

Dan heard distant shouts, and then, in a new sudden silence, the engine of a car.

Things were not better but worse.

The man had tools. Or had had. Dan pulled out his pencil flash. It didn't work. He had broken it, diving into the brambles. He groped between the strands of barbed wire. He saw, just barely saw, that the man on the other side was on his hands and knees, grunting and spitting. Dan wondered if he had broken the man's jaw, or cracked his skull, and whether he would go to prison for that too, if he was still alive, when this was all finished.

Headlights glared. The searchlight was switched on again. The car came fast along the road instead of slowly.

Dan climbed the fence. He did not like doing it in the dark. He was in a tearing hurry, but climbing barbed-wire was not a thing to do in a hurry. Brambles grabbed at him, threatening his precarious balance. He was utterly helpless on the fence if the man on the ground recovered quickly, or the car came up quickly with its searchlight.

It was coming up quickly. The searchlight glared like the eye of a malevolent god. The man on the ground was faintly illuminated by the approaching light. So was Dan. The man saw him. He shouted wordlessly, and grabbed at Dan's legs on the barbed wire. Dan jumped and rolled away. At the moment he did so the car screamed up to the place and the searchlight glared at the fence. Dan was on the verge of the road, on the same side of the fence as three or four men, a gun or more than one gun, and Eddie Birch. But the grass of the verge was very different from the brambles of the wood. Dan rolled, holding his stick and billhook close to his body. He felt that his trousers were in tatters from the brambles. He had further torn his leather jacket and his arm in his jump from the high barbed-wire fence. He had lost his cap. He had no idea which side of the fence it was.

The cap was not identifiable. But two men had seen his face full in the light of the lantern.

Rolling and then crawling, Dan made a little noise. Not much, in the mist-soaked grass. Not enough to be heard over the voices and the footfalls of the men.

The searchlight was swinging wildly to and fro, up and down. The man Dan had hit tried to explain what had happened. He did not know what had happened. Eddie Birch raved. Dan had seen the possibility of violent anger in his face at the gymkhana, and when he was insulted by Miss Trixie Hadfield; now he heard the anger. It was directed not at Eddie Birch's own men, but at Dan. Except that, for the moment, praise God, Eddie Birch did not know that it was Dan he was angry with.

Dan crawled until it was safe to run. Then he ran.

He ran far and fast, and then squatted under a hedge to get his breath back and collect his jumbled thoughts.

What would Eddie Birch think? What would he do? What was Dan to do?

By now Eddie Birch would have a description of Dan. It might be a good one. It might even be enough for him, with what he had himself seen at Albany, to identify the Hadfields' odd-job man as the intruder. On top of this, Dan had been seen at Albany by the men with the caravan, the tree-fellers. He had been seen from the window of the cottage. They might think he was snooping. He was linked to the Hadfields. If he was on their side, he was Eddie Birch's enemy.

What did Eddie Birch do to his enemies? What did he do to the crippled mothers, the animals and birds, of his enemies?

As to Dan, he was exactly where he'd been when he started out, except that his clothes and much of his skin were in shreds. He had all the same problems. He faced all the same choices of evils. He still had to get in, find the Surrey pony, get himself and the pony out again. Until this was done, nothing else could be done.

He had to try another place, more carefully, without wire-cutters. The pony would have to leave by river, as there'd be no gap in the fence.

The prospect was dreadful. Prison was worse. There was no third option.

Dan prowled back along the road towards the Albany boundary. This was not, he thought, what Eddie Birch would expect him or anybody else to do. But Dan was wrong. Eddie Birch did expect his return. The car was parked on the verge just beyond the end of the property, where the road curved away from the river which almost encircled the land. The engine was ticking over softly and the searchlight was on. The searchlight raked the boundary fence, lighting the edge of the wood almost as far as the lane. The mist hampered the searchlight, but not much. It was a very powerful searchlight with a concentrated beam. It would pick out a beetle on a blade of grass. It was not being swung in any sort of consistent rhythm. Had it been, Dan thought he could have predicted moments of darkness as with a lighthouse on the coast, and nipped across from cover into cover. But the man manipulating the searchlight was using his head. There was no pattern in the swings and swoops of the beam. Dan was as likely as not to be caught in it as he crossed from the fields into the edge of the wood.

There was another bright light by the lane, where the caravan was parked. Dan went softly and circumspectly towards it, keeping well away from the road and the searchlight. What they had at the mouth of the lane was a floodlight fixed high in a tree, a tree they had not felled, shining down on the trees they had felled. It glared down on the caravan and the car, and on the huge tangled obstacle of the felled trees, and on the barbed-wire fence each side of the mouth of the lane.

Beyond, the road rejoined the river a short way on — the road almost straight, the river curling back on itself. As Dan expected, another car was down there, with another searchlight.

It was still legal, all that Eddie Birch was doing. (Except, maybe, mounting a searchlight on a car. Dan had an idea that was frowned on. He warmly agreed with the frowners.) But it was weird — it would seem extraordinary to the police and to everyone else. On a building site, yes — outside a factory or a warehouse, yes — these tremendous and obvious precautions made sense. But to guard a few acres of useless scrub as though it was a diamond mine? How would Eddie Birch explain if anyone asked? And surely somebody would ask? The lane was used, though not much. Willie Martin used it if he went from Yewstop to Milchester. Not at this time of night, to be sure. Would Willie Martin see the distant glow of the lights? Would he come and enquire? Would he report it?

If the police came and investigated, they'd go on and poke round

Albany. They'd spot the Surrey grey pony. Miss Trixie would be asked about it, if she was still alive and still there. She'd say what she had to say, in order to clear herself . . .

Making a detour round the floodlight, Dan prowled on, eastwards, parallel to the boundary fence. He looked at the other car, at the handling of its searchlight. The man swinging it was not as bright as his opposite number. He had lapsed into a rhythm. The movement of the beam was predictable.

Dan picked the optimum point to cross the road to the fence — a point where the glow of the floodlight had faded to comparative uselessness, which was also at the extreme range of the car's searchlight. With the searchlight pointing in the right direction, he would be seen, no doubt of that. Seen crossing the road, seen on the verge, and above all seen climbing the awkward five-strand barbed-wire fence.

He crawled to the edge of the road, opposite his chosen crossing place. He felt like an escaping prisoner of war. But he did not think Eddie Birch subscribed to the Geneva Convention. He waited until the beam had swung over his crossing place and swooped away. He reckoned he had a few seconds. He sped across the road and buried himself in a clump of half-trampled bracken. He waited until the beam had raked the place and moved on. He moved like a lizard to the fence, and curled himself round the base of an overgrown hazel-clump. The hazel was lit to a faint, fatal brilliance. Then it darkened. Dan sprang to the fence and climbed desperately over it. He avoided the third strand, in case the alarm warned of pressure as well as of being cut. He wanted ten seconds for climbing the fence; he had about three. One end of this section of the fence was stapled not to a solid tree but to another hazel. It bent under his weight: bent and swung and threatened to spreadeagle him over the strands of wire. He was hampered by his stick and his billhook, but he dared not leave either behind. He tore one of his hands and rent his trousers on the bars of the wire. He dived off the fence, into the wood, just as the searchlight returned. This time he dived not into grass but into brambles.

He was able to pick his way twenty yards into the wood at this point, the brambles being only knee-high. He was assisted by the faint intermittent glow of the searchlight. Soon he had neither light nor any possibility of getting through the brambles without the billhook.

Dan had done a great many different things, in woods, in the darkest hours of the early morning. He had poached all kinds of birds and animals; he had made love to all kinds of girls; he had hidden from gamekeepers and policemen and a few husbands. But he had never tried to cut a path through an ocean of brambles, with no light to help him, making no sound.

It was tricky. It was exhausting. It shredded within minutes what was left of his trousers and, it seemed to Dan, what was left of his skin. Even the tough leather jacket seemed to be flapping in tatters round his chest.

One thought pushed him on, drove him and his precious billhook through the nightmare of thorny tendrils: it was highly likely the police would come to Albany the next day, and, if they did . . .

Dan had no idea how long he took to cut his way through the brambles. It seemed to him that dawn must be approaching. Usually his head carried an infallible clock, but the confused and frightening events of the night had stopped the clock, or sent it mad. He did not know if it was three in the morning, or five, or later. He was conscious of the driving need to get on through the brambles, and of the repeated tearing of his tattered clothes and tattered skin.

The brambles thinned. They tripped him up, but they no longer threatened to engulf him. It was still difficult to get through them, in the dense misty darkness of the wood, but it was no longer a ceaseless struggle against an enemy with a billion snaky face-high thorn-encrusted arms.

Dan groped his way through the last of the brambles, and twenty seconds later felt against his chest the rickety post-and-rail of the Hadfields' outer paddock. He heard, and dimly saw, a dozen ponies. He wondered if he would recognize the Surrey grey in the dark, without his pencil flashlight. He realized that he had to get a head collar, or some kind of halter — ideally a bridle — for his swim with the pony in the river.

He found that in the dark he could identify the ponies, more or less. At least he could feel clumsy heads and big barrels: he was sure that none he investigated with his hands was the dainty grey from Surrey.

The pony he wanted was not in this paddock. It might be in another, or in a loose-box. It ought to be in. Miss Trixie understood that, Dan was sure, as well as he did. But she was by no means reliable. Or, to put it more exactly, she would give the pony's comfort a far higher priority than Dan's comfort.

Dan thought the pony was probably out, but he looked in the stables first. All the stalls and loose-boxes were empty. Dan listened intently outside each to be sure of this, since he had no light. He did not dare turn on any of the lights in the stables. After a few minutes he was sure there was nothing in any of the stables except straw, buckets, and a comfortable smell of muck.

Dan went to the tackroom at the end of the row of boxes. It was padlocked, but the key lived under a brick by a water butt. He slipped in and shut the door. There was only one small window, with a blind, on the side away from the house. Dan pulled down the blind, groped his way back to the door, and flicked the switch of the light. Nothing happened.

'Bulb's gone,' murmured Dan, annoyed.

Then a thought struck him — a thoroughly unnerving thought. If Eddie Birch could cut a telephone cable, he could cut an electric cable.

Dan groped for the row of pegs on which the Hadfields hung their halters and head-collars. To find a bridle that would fit the grey, by touch only, in the dark, was beyond him. But rope halters went any size you liked — you just pulled headstall and noseband tight through the loops of the rope.

He found a halter of soft nylon rope, and slid out of the tackroom into the stable-yard. Everything was dead quiet. There was no sound from the farmhouse. There hardly would be, at this time of night, even if the Hadfields were still there, even if they knew what was happening to them.

Dan shut the tackroom door and put the padlock back. He pushed the hasp of the padlock back into the works. As the lock engaged there was an unavoidable click, the first sound he had made. It sounded very loud in the stillness of the stable-yard.

Dan saw a brief flash of pale light from one of the windows of the farmhouse. He knew what it was. As he threw himself down behind the water butt he heard, a fraction of a second later, the roar of the old 16-bore shotgun. Shot slapped into the water butt. One pellet pinged into the rubber sole of Dan's boot, harmlessly.

It seemed the Hadfields were at home. They were alive. They might know what was happening to them.

Miss Hettie fired her second barrel. Her aim was wild. The handful of shot banged into the wall of the tackroom far above Dan's head. Some whanged into the guttering and ricocheted away.

Dan heard an exclamation of disgust. He heard Miss Hettie break the gun to reload it. He got out fast and safely round the corner of the stables.

The old ladies were making it difficult for Dan to help them, if that was what he was going to do. He imagined he was going to — as soon as he has sorted out his own problems.

He searched another pitch-dark, dew-drenched paddock, and prodded another dozen damp ponies, before he found the small classy head, the soft confiding muzzle, of the Surrey grey. He put the halter on the grey pony and led it to the gate into the garden of the cottage. It was a good gate, put there by the Morrisons — a far better gate than any of the Hadfields'. It swung open silently, clear of the ground. Theirs squeaked, and scraped, and were held shut by pieces of binder-twine. Dan crossed the grass between the dainty shrubs the Morrisons had planted — Eddie Birch's shrubs now. He kept well away from the cottage, remembering the twitching curtains in the upstairs window. He could see well enough in the dark to avoid running into things. His feet and the pony's made no sound on the wet grass. He whispered to the pony and stroked its neck and ears, hoping it would trust him enough to go into the water in the dark.

The gun went off behind him. Shot sang close by his hip. The bang was too much for the pony. It reared, pulling the halter-rope out of Dan's hands. It bolted across the garden. There was a crash of broken glass. The pony stamped, rearing. More glass crashed.

Cold-frames. The pony had jumped into the glass of the cold-frames which Dan himself had made two years before. It might cut its feet to ribbons.

'Don't shoot, Miss Hettie,' called Dan. 'Pony's liable to've hurt himself.'

They caught him and soothed him. Miss Hettie, as far as Dan could see in the dark, was wearing her normal working clothes, even to the bowler hat. She reloaded the gun as Dan held the pony and comforted it. He led the pony back to the stable-yard: Miss Hettie followed, keeping the gun trained on the small of his back. There was no sign or sound of anyone else, of Eddie Birch and his army.

Dan was not really frightened of Miss Hettie's gun, any more than he had been when they played this scene before. He could certainly get away in the dark. But, as before, running away solved nothing. All the problems remained. The was still a grey pony too many at the farm, a fact which, of itself, was highly likely to send him to prison and leave his mother on her own.

Besides, Dan badly wanted to know what was happening at Albany. And he felt responsible for whatever had happened to the pony. He did not mind pretending to be frightened of Miss Hettie's gun, because he was truly frightened of other things.

Miss Hettie lit a hurricane lamp in a loose-box. She looked Dan up and down with disfavour.

'Is that the proper order of dress for horse-stealing?' she asked coldly.

Dan looked down at himself. His appearance was even more wildly tattered and dishevelled than he had thought. His trousers were barely decent, so savagely had the brambles and the barbed-wire attacked them. The skin of his legs and hands was cross-hatched with scratches and smeared with blood. He imagined his face was as bad or worse. It felt worse.

The pony, by contrast, had only one serious cut, a gash on the off-fore shin. It was deep, and bleeding freely. It was hurting the pony. There was no question of the pony going anywhere for days — no question of Dan leading it or riding it away.

'You wicked boy,' said Miss Hettie Hadfield to Dan. 'You're really in hot water this time.'

8

Under Miss Hettie's direction, and under the muzzle of her gun, Dan bathed the pony's leg, puffed blue antiseptic powder on the cut, and wound a three-inch Elastoplast bandage over a pad of sterilized lint. Tied up to a ring in the stable wall, the pony stood quiet, as good as gold.

Miss Hettie did not stand quiet. She complained bitterly about the failure of the electricity.

'I suppose it is the miners striking again,' she said, 'or the power-station people, or whoever it is. We can't ring up about it, because the telephone's out of order too. Disasters never come singly. It never rains but it pours. It's all a perfect nuisance. The Land Rover is practically out of petrol, too. Not that it's any good to us, until the men get those trees out of the drive. Careful with that dressing, boy.'

Crouched by the pony's foreleg, Dan felt full of admiration for Miss Hettie. She had followed him, alone, three hundred yards in the dark. She was not frightened of anything. She was a soldier's daughter.

Still at gunpoint, Dan gave the pony a brick of hay from the loft. He started to fill a bucket from the standpipe in the yard. He expected the water to gush noisily into the iron bucket. But it dribbled.

'Hurry up, boy,' said Miss Hettie.

'Bent much water i' thiccy tap, ma'am,' said Dan, remembering to revert to the voice and manner the Hadfields expected of him.

'Another aggravation! I expect there's a blockage in the pipe. Probably something idiotic you've done. Or my sister. Come in and fill the bucket in the house. Turn that tap off, fool! Quick march. Lively now.'

With two inches of water in the bucket, Dan walked obediently to the back door of the farmhouse. He put the bucket under the scullery tap. There was a brief gush, then a gurgle, then a few more drops.

'What *has* Trixie been doing to the pipes?' said Miss Hettie crossly.

'Nothing,' said Miss Trixie, coming into the scullery with another hurricane lantern in her gloved hand.

Miss Trixie was dressed, like her sister, for a day's cubhunting, in breeches, boots, tweed jacket and bowler hat.

'Go and look at the tank, Dan Mallett,' said Miss Hettie, waving the muzzle of the shotgun at him. 'You know where it is, in the attic. No funny business. I'm just behind you. Take this lantern.'

Dan went up the stairs, which were not much broader than those of his own poky little cottage. The walls of the staircase were covered with pictures which, as a boy, he had studied for hours — watercolours of Indian life, photographs of polo and tent-pegging teams, of Colonel Hadfield with monster mahseer pulled out of huge Indian rivers. All the walls of the house were similarly encrusted. In the study there was a silver-framed photograph of the Hadfield sisters, as young girls, in riding-habits. They were not pretty girls.

Dan went up a ladder into the attic which was full of cobwebs, the droppings of bats, and leather trunks of the Colonel's clothes and sporting equipment. He crawled under a beam to reach the galvanized iron water-tank. It was empty.

Albany had a well, of course. But the water had been polluted some years earlier by seepage from an underground oil pipe. The pipe went from a 600-gallon tank to the Hadfields' boiler. With the well useless, the Hadfields had had main water laid on, which had cost them a great deal of money. Dan thought that was why they had sold the cottage.

Eddie Birch had cut off the main water.

Of course there was the river. Dan could fill buckets in the river, if Eddie Birch and his men let him. He could creep out in the dark with buckets. But it was a long way from the nearest point of the river bank to the farmhouse — a very long way to carry two full buckets. There was no water-cart on the farm. No doubt there had been one in the old days, but now there was no need for one. The troughs in the paddocks were filled by hoses from the mains. Another hot day or two and the troughs would be dry.

Could they take all the ponies to the river to drink? Would they be allowed to?

Dan went slowly down the ladder, Miss Hettie's gun pointing up his backside, until he reached the shabby carpet in the upstairs passage.

'Just as I said,' said Miss Hettie with gloomy satisfaction. 'Disasters come in threes. Nobody warned us about a drought. Nobody advises us to store water. Incompetent fools. Typical jack-in-office idiots.'

Miss Hettie had still not taken in the real situation.

Miss Trixie had. She said to Dan, 'That impertinent Birch seems prepared to go to all lengths. But I can't imagine what he thinks he hopes to gain by it. We are not going to sell our home just because we have to go without baths for a day or two.'

'An' food, an' drink?' suggested Dan. 'For a month or two, mebbe?'

'Nonsense. The shop delivers . . . oh.'

'They thenks ye ben an' oprooten t'Bedfordshire.'

'Good gracious, why Bedfordshire? We have no connection of any kind with Bedfordshire. It is not as though we had even ever hunted with the Grafton . . .'

'I suppose the whole country is on strike again,' said Miss Hettie, who was still clinging to her earlier theory. 'But we have no means of knowing what is going on in the world. The newspapers did not come yesterday. I suppose we cannot hope for them this morning. Without electricity the television seems not to work. The wireless—'

'I reminded you about a new battery a week ago, dear,' said Miss Trixie coldly.

'And then allowed me to forget that you had done so. It is pathetic, the way you always contrive to refuse to accept blame. A very childish streak.'

'Let me have a look at you, Dan Mallett,' said Miss Trixie, pointedly turning her stiff old back on her sister. 'Dear me, what a sight you present. However did you get your clothes into such a state? You never think of your poor mother. You are scarcely decent as you are. Those scratches should be disinfected. Come into the bathroom. Find the iodine, Hettie, and cotton wool, and sticking plaster.'

Miss Trixie made Dan strip to his underpants. She told him sharply to be brave, as she dabbed at him with the iodine. She covered him with the stuff, as he was deeply scratched all over his face and body. He looked like a skewbald pony. The iodine stung savagely in the cuts and scratches.

They found some clothes of the late Colonel's — stiff tweed trousers and a collarless flannel shirt. The clothes were far too big for Dan.

'Father was a six-footer,' said Miss Trixie. 'He put on weight latterly. We thought it right to keep many of his clothes. Now for heavens' sake, boy, look after those trousers. Don't treat them as you do your own, tearing them and spilling food too, I daresay. I shall expect them to be returned in the same condition as when you borrowed them. That is simple good manners. I am obliged to talk to you like this, as apparently no one else has done so.'

Dawn came. Everything looked as peaceful and pleasant as usual. The ponies were like ghosts in the misty paddocks. A few birds chattered from the woods. The grey pony looked out over the half-door of his loose-box.

There was a little food in the farmhouse. There was no means of cooking anything until Dan had laid and lit a fire in the drawing-room fireplace. Miss Hettie broke eggs into a frying pan balanced on the logs. There was no water for tea or coffee, and no milk. Dan was very thirsty, but there was nothing he could do about it.

'We'll manage,' said Miss Trixie. 'We'll call that insolent creature's bluff. In a day or two he'll realize that we can't be browbeaten.'

She went off to write letters. Dan did not remind her that there was no chance of the letters getting to the post.

Miss Hattie fretted about not being able to wash up after breakfast. Then she cleaned her shotgun.

'No more of your pranks,' she said to Dan, 'or I'll know what to do.'

Both sisters had been up all night. Both looked as tired as Dan felt. But their voices were calm, except when they quarrelled with one another. Dan thought of the Khyber Pass and the thin red line; he was not yet prepared to bet on the outcome of all this.

Shortly after nine a fist pounded on the front door of the farmhouse.

'It's that insolent man,' called Miss Trixie from the study. 'Don't let him in or talk to him, Hettie.'

'As though I should dream of doing either,' said Miss Hettie. 'I don't need to be told how to behave to a purse-proud Johnny-come-lately.'

An envelope was pushed through the slot. Footsteps receded.

Miss Trixie emerged from the study, ink on her cheek. She picked up the envelope as though it smelled, or was slimy to the touch. She tore it open.

'I write to apologize for any inconvenience my workmen are causing you,' [Miss Trixie read aloud]. 'I hope it will be of extremely short duration. I have a number of men busy here now, and will if necessary send for more in order to expedite the jobs that need to be done. Meanwhile I beg you to remember that we are always on the spot and at your service. Tradesmen will be able to deliver to the mouth of the drive during the period — hopefully brief — while the drive remains blocked. I am ensuring that there is always a man there to take charge of anything delivered to you.

'I suppose we must expect the first frost any day now. Fortunately my men are warm and comfortable in their caravan and can, of course, come and go to get any supplies they need. You will be glad to know that they have water and electricity, and can consequently remain here as long as we need them.

'Further to our recent conversation, I enclose a document which you will both wish to sign. I hope this is as satisfactory to you as it is to me. Yours faithfully, Edward Birch.'

'Faithfully, indeed,' snorted Miss Hettie. 'What is the creature's document?'

'We, the undersigned Miss Theresa Hadfield and Miss Henrietta Hadfield, being joint owners of the property known as Albany Farm, Medwell Fratrorum, near Milchester, do declare our acceptance of the offer made by Mr Edward Birch to purchase the said Albany Farm, all land and buildings pertaining thereto, all horses and ponies belonging to us thereat, and the business known and trading as the Albany Riding School, for the sum of one hundred thousand pounds, of which sum we hereby acknowledge receipt. We hereby instruct our solicitors, Messrs Cardew, Pratt and Wilkinson of Chancery Lane, London, to proceed with the conveyancing in accordance with our wishes as above clearly set forth, and to deal with such solicitors and/or estate agents as Mr Birch may appoint to act for him.'

'What's that other bit of paper?' asked Miss Hettie.

'A cheque,' said Miss Trixie, blinking at it. 'Made out to me. For £100,000.'

'Why to you? Why not to me? Or to us both?'

'It is academic, dear.'

''At's a clever letter,' said Dan, inspecting it. 'Sounds like nothin' 'cep' friendly. Threatenin's all between the lines.'

'Not when it is read out in court,' said Miss Trixie, 'to a jury who have been told the true situation. We shall go at once to the police to lay an information. Birch can cool his heels in prison for a few years.'

'Ay,' said Dan. 'Go t'police. Yes, ma'am. How?'

'We can't leave that pony,' said Miss Hettie. 'He has a very nasty cut. I want the vet to look at it . . . . Oh. How will he get here?'

'The police shall come here,' said Miss Trixie. 'Dan Mallet, you can do something useful for once in your life. Go and fetch some policemen. The more the better. They'll have our drive cleared in two shakes. Then we shall put Mr. Birch where he belongs.'

'Tell the policemen,' said Miss Hettie, 'not to blow those sirens they have on their cars. We don't want the ponies frightened into fits.'

'This Birch person must be demented,' said Miss Trixie. 'How could he suppose for a moment that he could get away with this —

this *banditry*, in this day and age? He must know we should send for the police.'

'No,' said Dan. 'He ben stoppen ye senden off, 'tes true. But he doan know I ben yere. He d' b'lieve ye can't send off. We ben one up.'

'Yes,' said Miss Trixie. 'You may be right, amazing as it sounds. You are, as it were, the joker in our hand. We shall play you. Go as soon as it gets dark, Dan, and fetch a squad of policemen.'

'And do remember,' said Miss Hettie, 'to tell them about their si-rens.'

'The man Birch thinks we can't send for the police,' said Miss Trixie. 'He feels safe. Even so he must be demented. Suppose we did sign his impertinent document. It would have no legal force, I take it, our signatures having been extracted by his threats. We should disown it the moment he let us out, and at the same time have him arrested.'

Dan had been thinking along the same lines. The point was glaringly obvious. It must be obvious to Eddie Birch. Therefore the old ladies were not going to be allowed out.

This point was obvious, too. It struck Miss Trixie as soon as it struck Dan, and Miss Hettie only a few seconds later.

'He is a cowardly bully,' said Miss Trixie hotly.

Her grey hair straggled out from under the bowler hat which, for some reason, she had put on to read Eddie Birch's letter. Her freckled old hands grasped a small riding-whip. Her eyes flashed from the wrinkled old face, which was flushed with indignation and resolve.

Libby Franklin was puzzled and alarmed.

In the small hours she had been woken by two shots from some way away, perhaps from the farmhouse. A few minutes later there had been another shot, much nearer. Voices. The crashing of glass. A pony. She could see nothing, peeping out into the darkness. She wondered if a pony had been shot, a burglar, one of the old women? Again she nearly telephoned the police.

She went back to bed — there was nothing else she could do — but it was difficult to sleep.

Mr Birch arrived in the morning. She told him about the shots, and about the stolen grey pony.

'Oh, the shots,' he said. 'That's one of the old funnies. Apparently she's famous for it. Imagining burglars, rapists, I don't know what. She's never hit anybody, but I gather it's a miracle she hasn't. I'm surprised they let her have a gun licence, if they do. Now, about this pony you saw. Are you sure it's the same? Can you be sure? They all look pretty much alike to me, but I admit I'm ignorant. It's the one you looked after? The one you gave the kids rides on? I shouldn't have thought the owners would sell, those snobs who sacked you like that. So maybe it is stolen, and the old bags are receivers. What a laugh. Of course the police will have to be told. Wait a minute. They were talking in the pub in the village, some of the locals. I wasn't paying much attention, but I remember now. There's a reward offered. The pony *was* stolen. I bet it's the same one. Well, the reward's yours.'

'I'll ring up the police now, shall I?'

'No.'

'But —'

'I still want to manage this deal calm and friendly. I want to get off to a good start here. No rows, no unpleasantness, like I said all along. Imagine the atmosphere if a police car full of bluebottles comes roaring up. And it's you who reported the pony. Horrible fuss, recriminations, everything I don't want.'

'Yes, well, that's why I didn't telephone the moment I saw him.'

'Clever girl. You did right. I'll go and see the police later today, in Milchester. That's the best way. I'll see the officer in charge, the top brass. I'll explain the whole situation. Don't worry, you'll still get the reward.'

'Oh . . . good. But the police will still have to come here.'

'Sure, but not today or tomorrow. The pony won't go anywhere. Those people can wait a day or two, the owners.'

'I'd like them to wait forever,' said Libby. 'I hate the idea of him going back to them. Couldn't we just — forget?'

'Oh no,' said Mr Birch, shocked. 'We must report a crime.'

Miss Trixie returned to her letters. She seemed satisfied that everything was under control. Dan would remain hidden all day in the farmhouse, so the enemy would be kept in ignorance of the joker in the Hadfields' hand. He would occupy himself in various ways. If he got thirsty he must be brave about it, and not whine and complain. When it was dark he must creep out, and run off for a policeman.

By noon Miss Trixie had finished her letters. She announced her intention of doing what her sister had done, but not yet she herself — she would march down the drive, inspect the barricade, and talk to the workmen.

She came back twenty minutes later, scarlet with rage and exhaustion.

'Why doesn't he kill us and be done with it?' she said, stamping up and down the kitchen in her bowler hat.

'Here's one good reason,' said Miss Hettie, waving her shotgun at the window.

'He could burn down the house, with us inside it.'

'But he *wants* the house.'

'Eddie Birch ben a-goen t'kip ye safe, ma'am,' said Dan humbly from a stool in a corner of the kitchen. ''Cause 'a need your mark t'thiccy paper.'

'Oh,' said Miss Trixie. 'A good point, Dan,' she added handsomely. 'We're safe until we sign.'

'But thirzty, ma'am.'

'Great Scott, yes. I'd sell my soul for a cup of tea.'

'A gin and tonic,' said Miss Hettie.

'Is there any tonic water?'

'The shop was going to deliver it today.'

'And gin?'

'That was coming today, too. I was going to telephone.'

'Luncheon will be somewhat dry.'

'Somewhat small, also. We shall be all right, but I'm sorry for a growing lad like you, Dan.'

'We must ration our supplies,' said Miss Trixie. 'Husband our resources.'

'Yes,' said her sister. 'How do you propose to husband six rashers of bacon?'

'The food in the deep-freeze will keep.'

'No, dear. The freezer is unfrozen. It requires electricity.'

'We shall eat what was frozen.'

'Yes. There is very little. It will do for tomorrow.'

'It is a pity we have no vegetable garden, or hens . . . There used to be an excellent kitchen garden, but nobody would come out here to dig it. Dan, you can bring us food and drink, when you return tonight with the police.'

'Ay,' said Dan guardedly.

'I have been thinking,' said Miss Trixie. 'All those brambles, and the barbed-wire. My father's trousers.'

Dan nodded. He had been thinking about the brambles, too.

'You must go away by river,' said Miss Hettie. 'Simply swim away.'

Dan said humbly that he could not swim.

'You *useless* boy,' said Miss Trixie, exasperated. 'Is there nothing you *can* do?'

'In the attic,' said Miss Hettie, 'there is a pair of water-wings. They were yours, Trixie. I remember Father getting them for you, because you were not a dab hand in the water.'

'They were your water-wings, Hettie.'

'Yours, dear. I swam very well, though so many years younger than yourself.'

'Then you swim the river,' said Miss Trixie, 'and fetch the policemen.'

'I cannot leave the injured pony.'

'I can take care of the pony.'

'I prefer to keep an eye on him.'

'You are frightened of swimming in the dark.'

'You will please take that back.'

They looked on the point of physical violence. To keep the peace Dan said that he would swim the river with the inflated water-wings and fetch the police, after nightfall.

'Can I help you?' asked Sergeant Marble in the Milchester Police Station.

'My name is Birch,' said the big fair man, whose tweed coat, heavy brown brogues and country hat all looked brand-new.

Mr Birch said that he had bought Albany Farm, with a hundred acres, outside the village of Medwell. He explained his family connection with the place. Sergeant Marble liked the story, although he did not understand why Mr Birch was telling it. Mr Birch's too-new country clothes would soon be decently weathered, especially as he had bought all the Misses Hadfields' ponies.

Sergeant Marble knew the old ladies. He had several times been out to the farm, or sent men there, because the Hadfields had reported burglars and horse-thieves. They were pests, the old girls, both of them. Funny in a way, and with plenty of guts, but trouble-makers. On the whole Sergeant Marble was glad to hear that they'd sold up and gone away, especially as they'd sold to this friendly bloke from London.

'They did warn me,' said Mr Birch, 'about thieves and vandals. They say they've had a lot of trouble.'

'They haven't, but we have,' said Sergeant Marble.

'Well, I admit I thought it was all imagination, but I don't think so now. That's why I'm here, telling you all this. The place is terribly isolated. Of course that's its charm. But it does make me vulnerable. I've got young kids, and I've got all those ponies. Adding some more of my own, rather a pricey batch. The point is, I gather there has been a valuable pony stolen locally —'

'Quite right, sir. Not far from your place.'

'I've got some workmen there now, blokes doing some fencing and forestry, and they caught somebody breaking in last night. He got away, unfortunately. He cut the wire, new wire I'd just put up. He could have climbed over, but he cut. The only reason he'd do that, it seems to me, is to get a pony out.'

'Could be. What do you want us to do about it, sir?'

'Nothing. I'm what you might call keeping you informed. Has anybody reported a lot of lights and noise at my place last night?'

'No. The only people you'd disturb is the folk in the cottage, that little place beyond the farm.'

'I've bought that. I wanted all my ancestral acres.'

'Then it seems to me, sir, you don't have to worry about disturbing nobody.'

'Good. I've got some lights on the boundary fence, the one on the road, and as I saw a few blokes patching up fences and clearing and suchlike. We had a bit of a hue and cry last night, but our bird flew away. Still, horse-stealing seems to be a bit of a local industry, and I guess there may be some commotion other nights.'

'You know the rule, sir — minimum force if you do catch anybody.'

'Sure. Anybody we catch, you'll get him in good condition.'

Sergeant Marble thought his visitor was over-reacting to the recent theft of one other pony and to finding one trespasser on his land. But it was a fault on the right side. The Sergeant reckoned that 80 per cent of thefts were easily avoidable if people only took a few simple precautions. Too many precautions were better than too few, and nobody was going to be disturbed because there were no near neighbours.

The Sergeant devoutly wished there were more people like Mr Edward Birch of Albany Farm.

'Time you were off, Dan,' said Miss Trixie Hadfield. 'Blow up your water-wings when you get to the bank. Put this little plug in the nozzle here, so the air doesn't all come out again. I hope you've got plenty of puff. Take off those trousers and roll them up, before you get into the water. Hold them up above your head. Keep them as dry as you can. They're very expensive trousers. All my father's clothes were extremely well cut and made of the finest materials. Come back with policemen and food and drink.'

'And remember to tell the policemen,' said Miss Hettie, 'not to use their sirens.'

9

Dan thought it highly likely that some sort of watch was being kept on the farmhouse. He also thought it highly like that he could elude the watchers. He went out of a downstairs window, to the surprise of Miss Trixie and Miss Hettie who expected him to use a door. He wriggled like a slow-worm towards the cottage and the river-bank. He was hampered by the stiff, antique rubber water-wings.

It was a colder night. The dew-sodden grass felt like iced flannel on his face. Eddie Birch was right — the first frost was due any day now. Dry days and cold nights would multiply the Hadfield's problems. They were used to their oil-fired central heating and their constant hot water. At their age, they needed both. They were tough, but they were not made of wood.

Wood, thought Dan. There was very little in the shed behind the farm-house. Of course there was an unlimited supply within a few hundred yards. Dan began bringing it in and sawing it up for the old ladies at this season every year. It was going to be very, very difficult to bring any in this year. If they needed warmth, they might have to sacrifice some furniture.

Dan crept among sleepy ponies, through thick clammy river mist, towards the cottage.

Owls were busy, both in the tangled woods and over the open pasture. The weird wild shriek of a white-owl, close over Dan's head, made him jump and bite his tongue. From a little way came the mysterious, melodious wail of a tawny-owl. Dan wondered why their voices were so loud when their flight was so silent. It was illogical — it was like a cat-burglar blowing a hunting horn to advertise his entry. He wondered how, in the clammy darkness, they could see field-mice and beetles and roosting birds. But they did. Now that their young were grown, they only hunted in the dark. Like Dan himself. He had great fellow-feeling for owls, and shared many of their habits, except for hooting.

Dan asked himself where he was going and what he would do when he got there. He was not going within miles of any policemen, not while the Surrey grey pony stood in that loosebox by the farmhouse. But what about the Hadfields? What about their horses? Heat and light? Food and drink?

Dan considered assembling a squad in the village, and taking on Eddie Birch and his London bruisers. But the idea only had to be examined to be rejected. Eddie Birch had already made himself known and liked the village. People were glad the farm had gone back to the family, and were not sorry to see the backs of the arrogant and unsociable Hadfields. As to assembling an army, even for the most innocent purpose, Dan would find it next to impossible. He was too much of a loner to have close friends, too dubious and secretive to be trusted. If he did raise an army and march it to Albany, Eddie Birch would bluff them, fob them off, send them away his friends and allies. Or, if there was a battle, Eddie Birch's mob would win it. They had the skill. They had guns. They had barbed wire, searchlights, and the oceans of brambles. If there was mayhem, there would be talk. Word would get to the police, who'd come out to the farm and inevitably see the grey pony.

Dan did not like leaving the old ladies, even for a few hours. They thought they could look after themselves, but they couldn't, not really, not if Eddie Birch mounted a proper assault. Probably he wouldn't yet, he wanted the Hadfields' signatures on a piece of paper. He wanted to be legal occupier of Albany. But he might lose patience, lose his temper, crash in. Then all the old ladies' guts, and Miss Hettie's gun, wouldn't save them.

And then, sooner or later, the police would come and see the grey pony.

Dan could get away without great difficulty by land or water. Getting back with the police would be easy. Getting back without the police would not be easy at all, if he was burdened with food and drink. Another midnight struggle through the brambles was an intolerable prospect.

But, if Dan did get out, he had to get back. He had to protect the Hadfields. He had to bring them food and drink. Pretty soon they had to have water and heat and light and the telephone. He had to get out; he had to get back; he had to have a reason for not bringing the police with him.

Not for the first time since this weird situation developed, Dan had not the slightest idea what to do.

He slipped through the post-and-rail which separated the top paddock from the grounds of the cottage. Someone was there, or had been. There was probably food. The cottage was burglarproof, but it was not Dan-proof.

The cottage was completely dark and silent. If anyone was there, he either went to bed early or was lying doggo deliberately.

Up against one side of the cottage nestled a shed in which the Morrisons had kept their expensive London-bought garden tools. It was likely to the point of certainty that the tools had been thrown in with the sale of the cottage. They were not things the Morrisons would want in a London flat; they were things Eddie Birch would want for his family country home. Among the things in the shed was, or had been, a three-piece extension ladder long enough to reach the top of the roof of the cottage.

The door of the shed was secured by a massive padlock. The key hung, or had hung, on a nail in the kitchen. Dan betted it was still there. Without it, as far as Dan was concerned, only dynamite would open the padlock. He had no sophisticated burglar's equipment and no skill with picklocks or skeleton keys. He was an amateur in that area, a beginner, although he was an experienced professional in other areas.

What the shed had, which only Dan knew about, was a removable board at the back. It was removable because Dan had taken out the screws one rainy day when he had sheltered in the shed for an hour, while patching the post-and-rail fence. This was not extraordinary prevision. He had not anticipated the need, one chilly autumn night, to get the ladder out and burgle the cottage for food. It was simply that loose boards in sheds, known to him and to no one else, were occasionally useful. This was something he had learned long before, and which experience had from time to time verified.

Dan crept to the back of the shed. His fingers, light as moths, groped for and found the removable board. He removed it, making only a minute grating noise that might have been made by a gnawing beetle. He put it gently down on the water-wings. The resulting gap would have been too small for most men. He squeezed in through the gap, making only a noise like a mouse with a cob-nut.

He was now knee-deep in forks, wheelbarrows, rotary mowers, fruit-netting festooned about the shed like cobwebs, scythes, rakes, hoes and a jumble of other gear.

There might be a platoon of men in the cottage. It might be Eddie Birch's barracks for part of his army. Dan might be trapped in the shed among tumbling hoes and hay-rakes.

The darkness in the shed was absolute. It was dense, enclosed, compressed, as though the last dim glimmer of light had been squeezed out by the pressure of walls and roof. It was quite different in quality from the clammy darkness outside. There was a smell of damp, of tarred string, of motor oil, of mice, of spiders. The ladder, its three sections telescoped together, still lay along the floor, leaning against a wall which was the outside wall of the cottage. Gently, gently Dan began to ease it out through the hole in the back of the shed.

Libby Franklin woke with a start. She was not sure what had woken her. It was some sort of squeak or creak. She pictured the easing open of a door or the jemmying of a window. She pictured a powerful drunk clawing upstairs to rape her.

She listened intently, lying trembling in one of the twin beds in the main bedroom of the cottage. She had no idea what time it was. She had gone to bed early, because there was nothing else to do. It might be 11 or 2 or 5 in the morning. The noise that had woken her could not be innocent. There was no such thing as an innocent noise in the middle of the night in an isolated cottage.

The night was very black. Libby could hear nothing, inside the cottage or outside, except her own harsh frightened breathing, and the distant crying of some sort of bird.

Conceivably a pony had made a noise — jumped out of the nearest paddock into the garden and crashed into something. It was terribly unlikely. It had happened the previous night, but then there were people about. The old woman with the gun had let a pony through the gate. Libby had never known a pony with other ponies jump out of a paddock into a garden where it would be alone, at least in pitch darkness. They might jump into a field to join others, but not to leave others.

The noise might conceivably have been a fox, nuzzling the lid off the dustbin. Libby visualized the dustbin. It was plastic. The lid falling off would make very little noise, hardly enough to wake her.

A man had made the noise. Must have. Libby was frightened. She was alone and very lonely. She had slept many nights in the Coxes' big horsebox, but then she had ponies for company. Then she was not afraid of being raped or killed, but now she was.

There was no further noise, nothing except the occasional eerie cry of a bird. Libby wanted to pull the covers over her head. But the bed was where a drunken rapist would look for her. She got out of bed as quietly as possible. The springs creaked and the bed-clothes rustled. She was cold in her nightdress in the damp night air. She groped her way to the door. The floorboards creaked under the fitted carpet. She pressed her ear to the door, listening. The wood felt cold and a little damp. She turned the handle of the door and gently opened it. There was a small screech from a hinge. The tiny passage outside seemed even darker than her bedroom. There was no sound from downstairs, from anywhere in the cottage.

There was a noise from above. There was someone on the roof. Libby gulped. How many men? How big? Why were they there? How could they get in? All the windows were bolted, upstairs as well as down, except her own half-open bedroom window. Libby groped across the room and closed and bolted the window. Before she did so she heard again a faint scratching on the roof. She could see nothing out of the window. It was pitchdark and the air was clammy with fog.

It was a bird on the roof, or a cat. There were mice, rats, squirrels, just inside the roof. No. No bird or cat or rat or mouse or squirrel had made the noise which woke her. It was a man on the roof, a gang of drunken rapists.

There was nothing in the bedroom to hit anyone with, no weapon bigger than a hairbrush.

Libby found her flashlight on the bedside table. She crept downstairs, using the flashlight only once, briefly. She listened intently as she went, her heart thudding so that she thought it must be heard in the village. She was terrified of walking into someone's arms, of bumping into somebody coming upstairs, of falling into a trap. She was more terrified of facing the unknown empty-handed. Several of the stairs creaked as she went down. The noise sounded like a ragged volley of shots.

She crept into the sitting-room and groped her way to the fireplace. There was a big steel poker there, one of a set of heavy fireirons which lent an antique touch to the bright little room. Libby's fingers closed round the handle of the poker. It was extremely comforting. Hefting the heavy steel poker, she felt some of her courage return. She was a strong girl who took a lot of exercise; she could hit a man really hard with the big steel poker. She could bash his head in.

She crept upstairs again, holding the poker in front of her, listening for the man on the roof.

Dan inched the extension ladder up the slope of the cottage roof. It was heavy and awkward, especially in the dark. Unsighted, he had to judge the angle of the roof by instinct, memory and remote-control touch. It was impossible to prevent the top of the ladder, as he pushed it up, from scraping against some of the uneven old tiles.

But the roof had been insulated inside. The noise was really very small. The little scraping of the ladder on the tiles would sound like mice under the roof, or sleepy starlings roosting where they had nested.

Dan made every movement very slowly, and listened intently between movements. There was nothing to be heard from inside the house. There was no movement, light, sign of life. All the windows, upstairs and down, were closed. No doubt all were bolted with their burglar-proof catches. Dan felt a growing certainty that the cottage was empty. But he did not jump to any of the overconfident assumptions which had nearly scuppered him at other times, when he was younger and less prudent and less concerned about his mother. He had all night. He could use all of the dark hours that he needed. Although he was becoming sure that the cottage was empty, he would act as if it were full of armed gangsters. It remained a possibility that it *was* full of armed gangsters.

Dan went up the ladder more soundlessly than the ladder had gone up the roof. He went as delicately as though the rungs were made of spun sugar and the roof of thin glass. He listened as he went.

Part of the roof was made of glass. There was a small skylight by the single brick chimney, which lit a cupboard between the two bedrooms. Dan had no idea what the cupboard might once have been, but the Morrisons had run hot pipes through it, fitted it with shelves, and called it an airing-cupboard. There was no such thing in Dan's own cottage — wet clothes were dried on the kitchen range — but he knew about airing-cupboards from the houses of gentry and near-gentry.

The skylight was almost invisible from the ground. The two small panes of glass were inset below the level of the tiles, and it was in the shadow of the fat brick chimney. It looked very small. It was very small, but not quite as small as it looked. It was not intended to open, but only to give some light to the little airless cubicle of the cupboard. Anybody would have assumed that it was no way to get in — that it would have needed an Oliver Twist with modern tools to enter the cottage by the skylight.

But Dan had replaced a broken pane, using this same ladder, the previous April. He had found then that, with some help from a chisel and a screwdriver, the whole wooden frame of the skylight could be lifted clear, like a trapdoor. The gap it left would not have admitted a plump man. It was about the same width as the gap in the back of the toolshed when the removable board was removed.

Dan should have bolted or cemented the frame of the skylight into the room as soon as he discovered it could be lifted out. It was his clear duty to do so; it never occurred to him to do so. There was a chance that, one day, one night, he might want to get into the Morrisons' cottage. He might want to entertain a girl there, when the Morrisons were away; he might want to hide there. Knowledge of removable skylights was like knowledge of removable planks. It might never come in handy; it might come in very handy. It was not really treacherous to the Morrisons, because no one else would use it.

Dan lifted out the frame of the skylight with the two small panes of heavy glass in it. He made another mouse noise, a beetle noise, but no more than that. He propped the skylight against the chimney. A high wind would have blown it off, but in quiet weather it was safe there. Dan eased his legs, in the bulky tweed trousers, through the gap he had made between the tiles of the roof. He groped with his feet for the topmost of the slatted wooden shelves, where Mrs Morrison had kept sheets for the spare beds. The sheets were there. They had been thrown in with the rest of the things, with the garden tools. Eddie Birch could entertain.

Under the thick pad of the folded sheets, the slats of the shelf creaked like an old door opening. The shelves would not have held a heavy man, but they held Dan. He climbed down, in the pitch darkness, until his feet felt the linoleum floor of the airing-cupboard. There was another small creak as he lowered his weight on to the floor.

He groped for the door handle, and twisted it. There might have been a bolt on the outside of the door, but by the mercy of God there was an ordinary handle. Dan twisted the knob as slowly as the hand of a clock. There was no sound from the passage outside the door, or from anywhere. The hunting owls had fallen silent. Dan inched the door open. Still inside the airing-cupboard, he stood rock still for several seconds, listening. He edged himself out into the passage.

There was a blink of light, for a split second, on and off. It was a flashlight. Somebody was behind him, with a flashlight. Even as he ducked there was a shocking pain in his head, an explosion of light inside his skull, then oblivion.

10

Libby crouched, aghast by the small crumpled body of the man she had just killed. The noise of the poker thudding the skull had been utterly dreadful — the noise of a spoon cracking a boiled egg, amplified a million times. Her fingers felt something warm and wet — blood — gushing blood from the split skull.

Libby did not want to look at the corpse. But she could not bear to be alone with it in the dark. Her instinct was to run into the bedroom, jump into bed, and pull the covers over her head. But she thought that would be cowardly and unsporting. She could do nothing for the corpse, but she could not leave it in the dark, crumpled in the door of the airing-cupboard. That would be improper, disrespectful. The corpse, she thought confusedly, ought to be laid out on a bed with pennies on its eyes. She shuddered at the thought of doing that. Blood would get everywhere, on to everything.

You were not supposed to move bodies. The police came and took photographs and tested for fingerprints. They arrested the murderer. She was the murderer.

No — not at all — she was defending herself. What against? Who against? A little old man? A young boy? She had only seen her victim from behind, and only for a tiny time as she blinked her flashlight on and off. He might be innocent. The village idiot. A messenger from Mr Birch. A schoolboy friend of the people Mr Birch had bought the cottage from. She had murdered him, hitting out in panic with all her strength. His skull was split and his blood was all over the passage carpet.

Libby began to tremble violently with cold, shock, horror, and an appalled sense of the trouble she was in.

'Christ,' said the corpse.

Libby screamed. She almost fainted. She switched on the flashlight, but the beam waved madly about the cramped little passage owing to the shaking of her left hand. She dropped the blood-smeared poker from a right hand which had lost the strength to hold it.

The corpse sat up with a groan. Libby recognized the groom with the amazing blue eyes. His small, brown, wedge-shaped face twisted into a grimace of pain as he touched the back of his head.

Libby felt a wave of relief which almost picked her up and washed her along the passage. She felt she could fall in love with the man simply out of gratitude to him for being alive instead of dead.

'I thought I'd killed you,' she said shakily.

'I thought so too,' said the groom. 'Reports were exaggerated, as the man said. Oh, it's you. Put you in here, did he, as part of the siege-works? It's very nice to see you, or would be if I could see. What did you slosh me with? Is that a poker? What did you think I was — a fire?'

I thought you were a burglar,' said Libby, 'or . . . something. I still think so.'

'Well, I thought the cottage was empty.'

'That's no excuse for burgling.'

'Oh, there's nothing here worth burgling. Even if I was a burglar. Unless Eddie Birch brought in a lot of silver?'

'Then why did you come? How did you get in?'

'Crack in the roof. These old buildings. I'm not much thicker than paper.'

Libby inspected him in the somewhat steadier beam of her flashlight. What he said was untrue. His waist was slim and his bones were small, but his shoulders were quite broad. There was nothing emaciated about him. He was wiry rather than skinny.

Suddenly he smiled, full into the beam of the flashlight. The beam wavered again madly, owing to the effect of his smile on Libby. He was dressed in the most ridiculous clothes, clownlike, surrounded by folds of baggy tweeds and flannel: there was blood all over the back of his head; and his broad, sweet smile seemed to melt most of the vital organs inside Libby's own ribcage.

'Why did you come?' she asked, trying to be stern, but feeling an answering smile, involuntary, threatening to split her face.

'Hunger and thirst,' he said mildly. I've been on starvation rations. The old ladies have turned nasty. Won't give me anything, because I told them they ought to sell out to Eddie Birch.'

'But . . . but . . . why do you have to stay there? Why do you want them to sell? Why won't they feed you? Why can't you go and get food in the village or somewhere? Shall I do something about your poor head? Shall I bathe it? Should it be disinfected? How do I know I can believe you? Whose side are you really on? Why are you wearing those idiotic trousers? Why do you sometimes put on such an extraordinary accent?'

'Ask me one at a time,' said the groom, loosening Libby's joints by smiling again. 'We'll get on better.'

'The first thing to do,' said Libby unsteadily, 'is bathe that head. And then, if you're really starving, I'll get you something to eat.'

She led the way into the glossy little new bathroom. He said he was perfectly well able to walk; but she wanted to pick him up, cuddle him, and carry him. She still felt overwhelmed with gratitude to him for being alive instead of an embarrassing and troublesome corpse. She felt a good deal more than that. She felt an enormous curiosity about him. He was not like anyone she had come across before, an extraordinary mixture, a member of a race apart of which, probably, he was the only representative.

The bathroom had a blind as well as heavy curtains. Libby risked the light.

'Why the blackout precautions?' asked Dan Mallett, whose name, which she had just learned, seemed to Libby to suit him perfectly.

She explained that Mr Birch wanted her to stay hidden and invisible in the cottage, so that the two old women at Albany would not get enraged again.

'He wants a — an amicable atmosphere,' she said. 'He wants it all on a friendly basis. It's very sensible of him, I think. He's being very patient, after the way they treated him. And after the way their father treated his father.'

'You haven't been out and about, then?'

'No, not at all.'

'Ah. Then you don't know anything about . . .'

'About what?'

'The workmen. Fencing, caravans, lights. Telephone and such.'

'This telephone is all right.'

'You don't know anything. Gum, what a relief that is.'

'Why? What is there to know? What do you mean?'

He would not explain, but smiled and bent his head over the basin.

Libby bathed his head with cotton-wool and Dettol and warm water. As she did so, she found that she felt more than gratitude, more than curiosity. His childlike eyes. The friendly, innocent lechery of his unnerving smile. His light-framed body and brown wedge of a face, his untidy mousey hair and narrow brown hands — all this and more struck her at the little gymkhana, struck her more forcibly than she had realized at the time. The impression he made on her had lodged inside her and grown.

Libby put a pad of lint over the cut, then wound a bandage round her patient's head. Her fingers tingled at the contact with his neck and brow.

She wished she had a smarter dressing-gown than the old blue cotton one she was wearing.

'There,' she said at last. 'How does it feel?'

'Honoured,' said Dan. He stood up and turned to face her. He was exactly the same height as she was. They were close together in the narrow gap between the bath and the washbasin. His amazing blue eyes were inches from her own.

He smiled. He said, 'Thank you very much,' and kissed her.

Libby was not a sophisticated girl, not widely experienced. She was not a tart. But she was not inexperienced either. She was very, very choosey. She was choosing Dan. His kiss was unlike any other she had ever had. It was exceptionally gentle, yet it was charged with a million volts of electricity. Libby shut her eyes, and wobbled, and responded happily.

'I'm sorry I hit you,' she murmured wildly into his cheek.

'You showed terrific guts. You're a great girl. Can you cook too?'

They disentangled themselves from each other, and went down to the kitchen. Blinds and curtains blacked it out pretty well. Libby felt suddenly hungry, and cooked a big plateful of bacon and bangers for both of them. She made coffee. They sat side by side at the kitchen table. Dan's table manners were far better than those of her late employer Mr Cox — than Mr Birch's, too, come to that. So was the way he spoke. She was more than ever puzzled by him — a man of obvious education, dressed like a clown and working as heaven knew what.

'What *do* you do?' she asked him, her mouth full of sausage and coffee.

'Bit of everything,' said Dan.

She tried to cross-examine him about himself and his life. She really did want to know the answers. But she found herself somehow inveigled into giving her own autobiography. It was very dull, she thought, but he seemed interested. He wanted to know what she aimed to do, how she hoped to go about it.

She told him about Mr Birch's plans, and her own part in them. She said how much she liked the two children, how strongly she approved of their father's ideas about them, how much she admired the way he had pulled himself up in the world and come down here to regraft himself on to his own roots.

And, of course, Mr Birch was a godsend to her — the answer to all her prayers. He was going to give her exactly the life she wanted — the chance to do the one thing she was good at. She was going to repay him by working like hell and making a big success of the riding school.

Dan pushed away his plate, sighed, and grinned at her. She felt herself grinning back. She thought: I am a tart after all.

He put his arm round her shoulder, drew her towards him, and kissed her. She felt his hand slip inside the front of her dressing-gown. She threw her arms round his neck.

Dan found himself unexpectedly moved by this girl. She was very attractive. Her body was all that he had guessed when he saw the free vigorous movements, the curves inside jeans and T-shirt. Her personality was simple in the best sense. She was really nice, nice all the way through.

This created the problem. Libby had decided to be loyal to Eddie Birch. She knew nothing about the siege. Dan had been shocked and disappointed to find her here, standing over him with the poker at her feet, because he had assumed — naturally assumed

— that she was in on Eddie Birch's plans, part of his army. But he realized almost at once that she knew nothing. Eddie Birch had kept her here, lying doggo in the cottage, precisely in order that she should know nothing. She knew nothing; she was loyal to Eddie Birch and his children. What Eddie was planning suited her down to the socks, but that was not the only reason or the main one. She would hear no ill of Eddie Birch. She wouldn't believe about the seige, the threats, not in a million years, not unless she was made to see it all. Probably nobody would find the situation easy to believe. It *was* extraordinary. But Libby least of all.

Consequently he had to deceive her. He hated doing it, but it was needful. It was necessary that she trusted him. That trust, properly used, created a supply of food and water for Albany, without which the old ladies were beaten. It created, maybe, an unwitting agent in the enemy's camp. At some stage, Libby must be made to see what was really happening. It would be a horrible jar for her. She would be furious with Dan for having lied to her. He would lose her for sure. That was a very great pity. All the same, he must lie to her, even as they lay naked and affectionate in bed together, because it was the only way out of this perilous mess.

Dan said there was a pony with an injured leg at Albany, and he could not leave it. The old ladies had antique, superstitious ideas about veterinary science. They'd put herbs or wood-ash or rotted cabbage-leaves on the wound, instead of sulfanilamide and sterilized dressings. This tied him to Albany. But the old women had turned against him because he had turned against them.

'People like my mother call the farm Birch's as often as they call it Albany,' said Dan. 'It's right that the name should come right again. Anyway, those two are too old. They must get out and retire. The ways things are, it's not fair on the ponies or the kids who come here to ride them. That's why I come here when I can, to keep an eye on things, whenever I find time.'

'Time from what, darling?'

'My trades. I'm jack of them all.'

'You're very small to be so useful. I know what you are. You're a bee, a honeybee. You're small and brown, and you make a nice buzzing useful honeybee, but you've got the most dreadful sting . . .'

She gulped, and her body moved against Dan's flank. He began to caress her skin with his fingertips.

He felt treacherous as he made love to her again.

Dan climbed the ladder and replaced the skylight. Libby promised to say nothing to anybody about the skylight. Dan knew he could trust her. He felt guilty all over again, knowing he would get only the truth from a girl he was lying to.

Libby helped him close up the sections of the ladder. They put the ladder away in the toolshed. It was easier putting the ladder back than getting it out, because Dan found the key of the toolshed on its nail in the kitchen.

When he put the removable board back into the toolshed wall, Dan stumbled over the water-wings.

'What on earth are those?' asked Libby, blinking her flashlight on them.

'Support for non-swimmers,' said Dan. 'Old style.'

'Not much support. Look, it's split all down the side. It's a good thing you didn't try to swim with them.'

'It is,' agreed Dan solemnly, thinking of the black cold waters of the river closing over his head.

She gave him bacon, fruit, a loaf of bread, some chops, a packet of frozen runner beans, all in a plastic bag from a Milchester supermarket. He filled a big plastic water container which the Morrisons had used for picnics.

'Don't the old bags let you drink either?' asked Libby, much shocked.

'They're hard,' said Dan. 'Powerful hard.'

They agreed on a signal — short-short-long-short-short, tapped on the sitting-room window. Dan said he hoped to call the following night. Libby said she hoped he would.

They embraced passionately. Dan picked up the old waterwings and started creeping back towards the farmhouse.

The sky was beginning, just perceptibly, to pale. The autumn river mist was dense and clammy. It was too early and too cold for any birdsong.

It was hard to keep the plastic bag from rustling. Dan went back circuitously, moving with the utmost caution. On his way he checked the troughs in the paddock. That in the paddock nearest the cottage was almost empty. That in the larger paddock by the farmhouse was completely empty. The metal was damp to his fingertips, from mist and dew; damp metal was no good to thirsty ponies. The old ladies would need all the water in his plastic bottle. He could get no more until nightfall. Perhaps not then, if Eddie Birch tightened his cordon or moved Libby out of the cottage or someone else into it. Reluctantly, worried about the ponies, Dan kept the top screwed on to the water container. He wondered how long this could go on.

Libby remembered, with a jolt, that she could have asked Dan about Hector, the Coxes' pony she had seen in the Albany paddock. He'd know how the pony had got there.

A suspicion was born in her mind. It grew rapidly, and turned into a certainty. Libby was sure Dan had stolen the pony from the Coxes and brought it here. A man who broke in to steal food would steal ponies. A thief was a thief. Libby's lover was a common criminal.

A most uncommon criminal, she thought, smiling tenderly into the darkness. She was glad about the pony. Dan was keeping an eye on it; soon she herself would have charge of it again. Mr Birch needn't be bothered about it. He needn't be bothered about Dan, either.

'You *useless* boy,' said Miss Hadfield, pointing her shotgun at Dan's stomach. 'Where are the police?'

Mutely, Dan showed her the slit in the side of the water-wings.

He decided not to tell the old ladies about Libby. They would jump to conclusions about Libby's part in the siege — wrong, but inescapable. Miss Hettie might try to shoot Libby through a window with her gun. If they somehow broke or bullied their way into the cottage, they'd use the telephone to call the police. The police would come and find the Surrey pony, and Dan would go to prison for stealing ponies and clocks.

So he said he had broken into the Morrisons' cottage and borrowed some food and water. He had hit his head getting in, and bandaged it himself. He had tried the telephone, but it had been cut off like their own. He said the cottage was empty but Eddie Birch had laid in some supplies.

'The thought of that man as a neighbour,' said Miss Trixie, 'makes me feel quite ill with rage.'

The old ladies criticized the quality of the food Dan had brought. They said the bacon was too salty, the bread stale, the fruit unripe, the chops fatty. They were suspicious about the purity of the water. They accused Dan of making the split in the water-wings.

'Carelessness,' said Miss Trixie.

'Mischief,' said Miss Hettie.

They attained an unusual level of agreement in their sniffy disapproval of Dan.

In a low, slow, treacly rural voice — unrecognizable as the voice of the man who made love to Libby — he told the old ladies about the empty water troughs in the paddocks. They did not believe him at first. They believed him in the end. They fell silent. Their faces, in the strengthening morning light, showed the greyness of worry and sleeplessness. They were too old for this sort of thing. Their health would crack, even if their courage didn't. And they were more concerned about the ponies than they were about themselves. Unless they could water the ponies, they might be forced to give in to Eddie Birch.

The ponies could be taken to the river bank, maybe, through the garden of the cottage. Or Dan could run a hose from the cottage to the troughs. He could coil the farm hose on a drum, roll it to the cottage, uncoil it again to the paddocks. Either of these ploys would have to be undertaken at night. Either would be hard to do in the dark, and almost impossible to do stealthily. Either would be quite impossible without Libby's help, as the old ladies were incapable of stealth. They were too old, too stiff, and too arrogant to creep.

Libby's help? She'd think he was crazy to water the ponies in the dark, either at the river or by hose. She wouldn't help — wouldn't understand the need to help — unless Dan told her the truth. She wouldn't believe the truth, unless Dan showed it to her. Showed her what? Some new fencing? Some felled trees? A blockage in the water-mains? A power cut? Eddie Birch could explain all those, and Libby would believe his explanation.

Suppose Dan got her to the farm. Suppose he proved to her that Eddie Birch was trying to starve and terrorize the old ladies into selling. Suppose he got her to believe it. She'd go to the police. She'd swim the river. No — easier — she'd simply telephone from the cottage. The police would come.

And see the grey pony, imprisoned now in the stable by its injured leg. And know that Dan had stolen it. And know that he'd stolen the clocks. And put Dan in prison. And leave his mother to fend for herself, with her arthritis getting worse every day.

In an agony of indecision and confusion, Dan settled himself for a nap in the little unused room beside the kitchen. The room had a bookshelf of pre-war novelettes, two grubby prints of racehorses (Hermit and Blair Athol) and one of Queen Alexandra, a strip of rush carpet on a brick floor, and a single shabby armchair with broken springs. Dan supposed it had been a servant's sitting-room, when the Hadfields could afford a servant. He sank into the armchair. The springs jangled. His head was aching. Just before he went to sleep, he remembered the golden moments of the night. He smiled as he slept, and had happy dreams.

He had an unhappy awakening.

Glass crashed and something thudded into the midst of erotic visions of Libby. Dan woke slowly. He had been terribly tired. He found glass all over his lap, over Colonel's Hadfield's tweed trousers. The broken glass was sticky with blood. The whole window had been broken, wood as well as glass, not just a single pane. Something big had broken the window, not a half-brick. What had? Where was it?

Dan blinked sleepily at the floor. A patch of bright sunlight from the east, from the clear cold morning sky, lit up the thing on the floor. Dan was almost sick. At his feet lay the severed foreleg of a pony.

11

A cheap brown envelope was skewered to the leg, as a price-tag is skewered to a joint of fresh meat in a butcher's shop. Blood had spattered the envelope. Blood dribbled on to the rush matting on the floor of the little bare sitting-room.

Miss Hettie burst into the room, with her gun. Miss Trixie was on her heels.

'What was that noise?' shouted Miss Hettie, pointing the gun at Dan.

She saw what lay on the floor, under the broken window. She paled, tottered, dropped the shotgun, and collapsed in a little heap on the floor.

Miss Trixie began to gag. She was near vomiting at the sight of the thing on the floor. She controlled herself with a tremendous and visible effort.

They were both desperately overtired. They had been under a strain which would have cracked many young men. Dan thought they were beaten.

Miss Hettie moaned and sat up. She was a bad colour. Her bowler hat had fallen off; her grey hair straggled out from her hair-net and wisped about her face.

'What a damned childish thing to do,' she said crossly. 'Never done such a thing before. Is that a letter?'

Dan pulled the little wire skewer from the pony's leg. He took a folded sheet out of the blood-daubed envelope, and handed it to Miss Trixie.

'My dear ladies' [read Miss Trixie in an exhausted voice], 'I am deeply sorry to have to report an accident to one of your ponies, a severe cut in the leg. I hope your ponies are insured, but even if they are I know you will be as distressed as I am by this accident.'

'Can't insure without a vet's certificate,' said Miss Hettie. 'Couldn't get one of them for any of the animals. Couldn't afford premiums, anyway.'

'What really bothers me' [Miss Trixie continued to read the flimsy typescript] 'is the possibility of another, similar accident, perhaps to an even more valuable pony than the first unfortunate victim. I hate to offer gratuitous advice to such experts, but even I can see that some of your fencing is dangerous and, I suggest, unsuitable for horses. I am aghast at the thought of a repetition of this morning's disaster, but until the stock is properly contained in safe fencing I cannot help feeling that more ponies are at risk. I think, in fairness to the ponies, I should point out that this dreadful occurrence does add some force to the suggestions I have already ventured to make to you. Hoping you will forgive this intrusion into your affairs, and into your grief, I remain, with best wishes, yours sincerely . . .'

'The beast,' said Miss Hettie passionately. 'The bloody butcher!'
'Clever letter,' murmured Dan. 'Like that other.'
Eddie Birch wanted the ponies, but he was prepared to sacrifice one of them to get Albany. One, and how many more? What horrible lump of meat would come next through the sitting-room or kitchen window?
There were sixteen ponies. Seventeen with the grey from Surrey. Eddie Birch could replace them, and with much better ones. He seemed to have unlimited money.
He could replace windows, too. Wood, glass, putty, paint and a few quid's worth of labour — it was peanuts to a man with his money, who could hire armies, butcher ponies, and offer £100,000 for a beat-up little farmhouse. There was nothing to stop him breaking every window in the house. And after the windows, the doors.
Dan glanced out of the broken window of the little sitting-room. He saw a clear, hard blue sky. It came through the gaping, jagged ruin of the window. It was cold. If the wind stayed in that quarter, a frost was certain. With its windows broken, the farmhouse would be chilly indeed. With the colder weather, the ponies would

need hay. Could Dan get hay out to sixteen ponies — fifteen — in the dark, undetected? He dared not show himself to Eddie Birch and his men by day. Neither one of the old ladies on her own could get all those bales down from the hayloft and out to the paddocks. They could do it between them — had done in the past, when Dan was unavailable. But if both old ladies left the farmhouse together, Eddie Birch would surely move in. They'd never get back. They couldn't get clear away, either. They'd sign the document, or die of starvation and exposure in their own paddocks.

'We'll bring all the ponies in,' said Miss Trixie.

'Are you mad?' said Miss Hettie. 'That man will set fire to the stables.'

'Nay,' said Dan, reverting to his broad, slow parody-voice in order to get them to listen to him. 'Stables ben old. Eddie Birch d'want un.'

'He can kill our ponies more easily,' said Miss Hettie tonelessly, 'if we bring them in for him.'

'Rubbish, dear,' said Miss Trixie. 'What's your gun for?'

'They must drink. They can get a bit of moisture if they're out. Dew on the grass. They're bone-dry if they're in. They'll go mad.'

They argued about it. Miss Hettie had a good point about the water. Even so, Dan thought Miss Trixie was right, on balance. He could get a little water, bit by bit, from the river or from Libby's cottage. It would not be enough, but it would have to be enough. He kept out of the argument; any contribution he made would only lengthen and embitter it.

The old ladies forced themselves to inspect the severed leg. They were not normally squeamish, but they were passionately fond of their animals. They argued about which pony had been butchered. They made themselves inspect the foot and the shoe. Miss Hettie said it was Samovar's foot; Miss Trixie was sure it was Goldcrest's. Dan knew both ponies intimately, and had done for a dozen years. They were very old, almost identical, almost valueless even to the Hadfields. Neither had ever hurt any child or other living creature; neither had an ounce of vice or ill-will. Having had nothing but kindness all their lives, both would go trustingly up to any man, whatever saw or axe he was carrying. Dan thought Miss Hettie was right this time, as Samovar had been shod more recently than

Goldcrest. It was profoundly unimportant. Either way it was sickening, monstrous, unthinkable.

Eddie Birch was mad, crazy. He was obsessed with getting Albany. He would go to any lengths of destruction and torture. Resistance — arrogant and contemptuous resistance — had goaded him to this horror, and would goad him to greater horrors.

But his madness was not of a kind that made him an ineffective enemy. It made him more effective, because it made him ruthless. The letter about the accident could be produced in any court. It would read well. It was written purely out of concern for the ponies. It was kindly, humanitarian. Between the lines, tactfully unstated, there was the suggestion that the Hadfields were no longer capable of looking after their ponies. Any policeman, any jury, would appreciate the merit of the suggestion, and the tact that left it unstated. And the letter was undated. It had been written days before it had helped persuade the Hadfields to sell the farm to this kindly, animal-loving man.

'If I'd ever had any thought of giving in to that swine,' said Miss Trixie, 'I'd give up the idea now. Fancy leaving our ponies in *his* care.'

Eddie Birch's idea had backfired.

Miss Hettie nodded. She was quite recovered. Her eyes were bright and her lips set in the ancient, weatherbeaten face. But they both looked tireder than ever. There was very little water. The house was cold. There was no water for the ponies.

'Tonight, you wretched boy,' said Miss Trixie to Dan, 'you *will* go to the police. We'll find a way. This cannot go on.'

'Prablem there,' said Dan slowly, 'ben thicky grey poany. Ef p'lice d'spy *two* grey poanies . . .'

'Borrowing a pony won't land you in prison, will it?' asked Miss Hettie.

'Borrowed a bit more'n the poany,' explained Dan. 'From the house where poany was. Folk name o' Potter. Ef p'lice d'spy poany . . .'

'They'll realize you took the other things at the same time, is that it? *Burglary?* I'm extremely shocked.'

Dan explained about his mother's arthritis, her need for a major operation, her utter refusal to go into a big ward in a National Health hospital.

'She d'say,' he finished anxiously, 'the doctors sneer.'

'She's absolutely right,' said Miss Trixie. 'They do sneer. Common little bounders, most of them. Not what I call professional men at all. Your mother is quite right to stay out of those big public wards. Infection everywhere. All kinds of people with all kinds of revolting diseases. She must go into a proper clinic.'

'Ben expensive,' said Dan.

'Which is why you felt obliged to take a few things from the — what are they called? Popkins? I've never heard of them. Newcomers, I suppose, another Johnny-come-lately lot, purse-proud ninnies from London, more money than sense *or* taste. I expect they had a lot of vulgar silver. That sort of thing is a dreadful bore to clean, and servants can't be trusted nowadays. They're better without it.'

'P'lice d'thenk defferent,' said Dan.

'Small-minded jacks-in-office.'

It was not at all clear to Dan where this conversation left him. The Hadfields, astonishingly enough, were not deeply shocked by his burglary. They understood why he needed money, and they didn't care what happened to rich newcomers in the village. They saw that he couldn't go to the police without disaster — disaster to his mother as well as to himself.

Disaster, conceivably, to Miss Trixie too. She might say she'd bought the pony in good faith from Dan. Would they believe that *she* could have believed that Dan had come by the pony honestly? How could he have?

It seemed they were agreed Dan couldn't go to the police. There agreement ended. What was he to do? Miss Trixie was right — the situation couldn't go on.

'It is clear what we must do,' said Miss Trixie. "We must turn defence into attack.'

The thought of attacking Eddie Birch made Dan feel a little sick.

Miss Hettie cooked the last of the food on the last of the firewood in the sitting-room fireplace. She used the last of the water to make three small cups of instant coffee.

The ladies forced themselves to eat, to keep their strength up. It was something their father had taught them. No soldier, they knew, could go into battle on an empty stomach. But they had to force themselves. The horror that had come in through the window had taken away their appetites.

After the meal, Miss Hettie wanted Dan to help her change the dressing on the grey pony's leg. Whatever nausea she might feel, just at the moment, about wounds on ponies' legs, she was clear that the dressing must be changed, and that Dan must help.

'No, dear,' said Miss Trixie. 'The wretched boy is still the joker in our pack. Birch and his gang had better not know Dan is here. I think it important that they remain in ignorance.'

Dan wholeheartedly agreed, especially as two of the gang had seen his face, full in the beam of their electric lantern, after he had cut the new wire.

Miss Hettie went crossly out to the loose-box on her own, her shotgun under her arm. Dan, peeping through a crack in a curtain, watched her from the dining-room window. No one bothered her. Eddie Birch wanted her signature. He thought he could get it without direct physical assault. He would cut off more ponies' legs. The time for cutting off Miss Hettie's leg would come later.

Miss Hettie reported that the grey pony was terribly thirsty.

Libby Franklin spent the morning in a trance. She did what she had never done before — she sat in an armchair in front of an electric fire for three hours, dreaming. Her dreams were filled by wide innocent eyes of cornflower blue, a wide childlike smile, and other things about Dan . . .

Mr Birch came on foot in the early afternoon. He seemed edgy, unhappy. Libby was worried. She liked and trusted him so much, she was so grateful to him, that she was upset to see him upset.

He asked if he might use the telephone.

'That's *ridiculous*,' said Libby. 'It's your telephone.'

'Oh no. While you're living here it's yours. This cottage is your castle. I'm your guest when I come here. Understood?'

She nodded, too full of gratitude to speak.

Mr Birch picked up the telephone and dialled a number Libby thought was London. She went quietly out into the kitchen: she had been brought up to leave any room where someone was telephoning, in case they wanted to say something confidential. But she could hear him, even if she tried not to. His voice was strong. He sounded impatient. He might have a bad line.

He said to the telephone that he needed more men again.

'Clearing's still incomplete,' he said. 'It's stiffer than I thought. Bloody obstinate, in fact. I need some more muscle . . . Yes, they'd better bring their own tools.'

He gave what seemed to Libby odd and complicated directions for the journey the men were to take.

Libby was surprised that he sent all the way to London for men to clear brambles from the woods. There were surely local men who could use slashers or even bulldozers. No doubt Mr Birch had good reasons, since he was a successful businessman.

He called her back into the sitting-room, and said he had been to see the police. 'About the pony, the one you say belongs to those visitors. It was stolen and there is a reward. The reward's yours, of course. A hundred quid. Any good to you? But I managed to persuade the bobbies to leave well alone for the moment. I explained the whole problem. I explained about my Dad, too, and why I was so keen to get the place back. They were very understanding, I must say — not a bit what I remember from the bobbies on the beat when I was a kid in the slums. How are you for food here?'

'Getting a bit low,' said Libby, remembering uneasily how much she had given Dan.

'You must have a hell of an appetite — there was enough to feed a platoon for a week.'

'Yes, well,' said Libby, as lightly as she could, 'I do eat like a pig, I'm afraid . . .'

'It's a good thing, they tell me. People who appreciate food appreciate other things too . . . Well, that's something for later, maybe.'

He glanced at her. She was a bit unnerved by the glance. He was attractive, in spite of his age; but Libby was a one-man girl, at any given moment, and at this moment the one was Dan.

She devoutly hoped nothing was going to happen to muck up her relationship with the Birch family — to muck up her own golden future with the Albany Riding School. It seemed possible. It was a thing that happened. You heard of cases.

Mr Birch left soon afterwards, friendly, powerful, calm, impressive. He told her more food would come. He told her to keep her head down. He told her that he was certain of buying Albany in the next day or two.

Sergeant Hallam of the Milchester CID had by no means given up hope of the stolen antique clocks. It was a peculiar case. It was definitely not the work of an ordinary professional villain, or even an ordinary amateur villain. The Old Mill, Mr Potter's house, had been left deserted for only a few minutes. Someone had slipped in — someone who was on the spot, someone who had inside knowledge. The same person had let a pony out of a horse-box, to create a diversion and empty the house. He had stolen another pony. It couldn't be two separate crimes with two unconnected villains at the same place and time. That was too much of a coincidence. Anyway, one of the two villains would have scared away the other.

The stolen pony had disappeared, as, to be sure, stolen ponies usually did.

All those clocks must have called for some form of transport. The Old Mill could be reached, by a car, only from the road and by its own metalled drive. There was no other way a car could get anywhere near it — no side-road, no cart-track, no back drive because of the river. Mr Potter and the others would have seen a car on the road if there'd been one. There hadn't. This was certain. None arrived, none left, none was parked, during the time they were out of the house. Yet during that time the clocks had gone, as well as the pony.

Therefore the pony had carried the clocks.

Of course such a thing was impossible. Everyone said it was impossible. The Super said it was the most idiotic thing he had ever heard of — a thief carrying eight valuable antique clocks on the back of a small pony.

Sergeant Hallam agreed that it was ridiculous, but he couldn't agree that it was impossible. Because no other explanation worked.

One man, in Sergeant Hallam's whole experience, was capable of a performance like that. Ridiculous, almost impossible, perfectly effective. That one man had disappeared. His old crippled mother, in the crazy little cottage under the edge of the Priory Woods, had been interviewed a dozen times. She said he'd gone out and not come back. He'd gone out, in the middle of the night, the night after the robbery. It was likely enough. The little bastard did his poaching and thieving in the dark. And now, not for the first time, he'd disappeared off the face of the earth.

Sergeant Hallman pictured Dan Mallett leading the grey pony, with eight antique clocks on its back, over the Wrekin or the Yorkshire Dales or the bogs of County Sligo. But that was ridiculous. Mallett wouldn't go far away, on account of his mother. So the Sergeant continued to ferret about in Medwell Fratrorum and its empty, sleepy neighbourhood. All he wanted was a sniff of the grey pony, or just one clock, or Dan Mallett. He went on talking to everybody; he went on searching everywhere.

He'd heard, from his uniformed colleague Sergeant Marble, about the pleasant stranger from London, Edward Birch, who'd bought back what was seemingly his family's old farm. Being a stranger, a new arrival, he wouldn't know anything. But he'd had some kind of trouble. He was worth a visit.

'Least,' said Sergeant Hallam to Detective Constable Stuckley, 'we'll likely get a cup o' tea from the bloke.'

'Or a drink?' suggested Stuckley.

'Mebbe. Combinin' duty wi' pleasure is a mark o' the superior mind.'

'Ow,' said Stuckley.

He turned the police car towards Albany.

'Wait a mennit,' said Sergeant Hallam. 'They 'ad a trespasser. Ketched un, but let un go. Wriggled off, likely. That were four o' the marnin'. They thoughted the bloke were after stealin' ponies.'

'It were Dan Mallett,' said Stuckley, 'seekin' t'hide they clocks in the brambly-bushes.'

'Yer. Which I wunner ef 'e done?''

They found the farm road into Albany blocked by felled trees. The trees had been trimmed, but the trunks formed a massive obstacle. Some workmen were squatting about them, taking things easy, drinking beer out of cans.

One of them fetched the Governor.

Mr Birch was apologetic about the trees. He said they'd be gone in a day or two, when a timber merchant came with a forklift. Meanwhile the only person inconvenienced was himself, and the inconvenience wasn't so very severe.

Yes, Mr Birch had heard about the stolen pony, and the burglary, from chat in the Chestnut Horse in the village. It was one reason he'd put up the new fencing the Sergeant could see. The farm was very isolated, and he had young kids and ponies of his own.

'Can't be too careful, these days,' said Mr Birch sadly. 'Vandals. Young lads, some of them. No parental control. Breakup of the family.'

'Quite right, sir.'

Mr Birch had not seen the trespasser on Monday night. But two of his workmen had. They were fetched. Sergeant Hallam didn't quite like the look of them, but that was Mr Birch's business.

Yes, they'd seen the bleeder clear. They described him pretty well, in funny London voices which Sergeant Hallam found difficult to understand.

It fitted Dan Mallett all right. So did creeping into somebody else's property at three in the morning, and getting away, and getting lost.

The two detectives searched the area where the man had been seen and the wire had been cut. There was nothing there except an old tweed cap buried in the brambles. Mallett hadn't gone further into the woods, not unless he'd flown or burrowed underground, on account of the brambles. Even a sneaky little bastard like Mallett couldn't get through that lot.

He hadn't dumped his clocks here, let alone his pony. He had come to steal ponies, likely, like Mr Birch said. He'd hoped to take advantage of an innocent new owner, fresh from London. He'd found more than he bargained for. Good job too. Pity he got away. When he was found, the two beefy-looking workmen would identify him. Then there'd be charges of assault, actual bodily harm and damage to property, as well as trespass.

Mr Birch promised to let the police know the minute anything happened they ought to hear about. He sent one of his men for a bottle of whisky and a couple of plastic cups from a caravan parked in the driveway. He gave them a drink. He was a good bloke. He'd be an asset to the neighbourhood, not like those old snobs who lived here previous. It was nice, too, that he'd come back to his family's old place.

Warmed by whisky and goodwill, Sergeant Hallam and Detective Constable Stuckley drove back to Milchester to report. A description of Dan Mallett was circulated (it was said that no photograph of him existed). A warrant was issued for his arrest.

After interminable argument, Miss Trixie said she would bring all the ponies in for their safety, whether Miss Hettie helped her or not. The argument was more rancorous than usual, because both old ladies were dead tired, nervy, frightened.

Miss Trixie could, in fact, perfectly well bring in all the ponies without help. She did not have to catch them all and lead one by one. If she put a halter on one in each paddock, the others would almost certainly follow. They might bunch and bump in the stable doors. That could be sorted out. They were very docile ponies, creatures of habit, accustomed to kindness.

Miss Trixie came back in four minutes. Dan was alarmed at her expression. Her face was angry, but there was a haggard look on it, a look of despair.

She said the gates of the paddocks had been wired up with turns and turns of barbed-wire. A strong man with heavy-duty tools could unfasten them, but she couldn't.

All the water troughs in the paddocks were empty.

The sun went down in a clear lemon-yellow sky. The air was absolutely still. It was, unmistakably, the night of the first frost.

12

Dan slipped, once again, out of a window of the dark farmhouse. It was dark because there was no way it could be lighted. There was only one candle left, and only two inches of that. There was no paraffin for the lamps. There were five matches left in the only matchbox. The battery of the single operative flashlight was getting dim and uncertain.

Dan crept away from the farmhouse, moving like a mouse with a guilty conscience. He saw that two men were on watch. If they were hiding they were doing it badly. One watched the front door, from the stables. Dan saw the glow of a cigarette. Another watched the back. Dan saw him clearly in the starlight, squatting against the side of the woodshed. Well, that still left a few, with lights and guns.

The night was clear and windless. Stars twinkled frostily out of a frosty sky. As Dan wormed his way to the cover of the ponies in the nearest paddock, he felt and heard the rough grass rustle and faintly crunch, starched by the frost to the fragile crispness of thin paper. The grass was cold to his hands and the air to his face. The white-owl shrieked somewhere near the river bank, somewhere near the cottage. Dan thought the Angel of Death must have such a voice.

As he crawled, Dan tried to weigh priorities in his mind. Everything was needed. Everything was urgent. The ponies needed water and hay. The old ladies needed food, fuel, light, heat, water. They needed matches, paraffin, firewood. They needed to be let out.

Most of all what was needed was an end to this situation. What end? Eddie Birch had pointed out that his men and himself could camp on the boundaries of Albany, in tolerable comfort, for ever. They could come and go as they liked, keep warm and fed, drink, sleep soft. What they were doing might look eccentric or extravagant; it wouldn't look evil or illegal. Far from it. Dan guessed

Eddie Birch had already had jolly meetings with the police, as he had with Bert Monger at the shop, Ted Goldingham in the Chestnut Horse, and probably half the neighbourhood.

Dan's own disappearance, after the theft of the pony and the clocks, must excite intense suspicion. Suspicion only of himself. Suspicion, but no surprise. The whole countryside would be looking for him, as well as the police. And looking for the grey pony, because of the reward.

An end to the situation. What end, other than the one Eddie Birch had in mind? Eddie held all the cards except one. Dan was still the joker in the old ladies' hand. He had won a small trick — some food and water. They were playing him again. It might well be their last chance to play. Their time was running out. Whatever their guts, neither they nor the ponies could stand much more.

The first thing to do was to supply the garrison. There was no more food to speak of in the cottage. Libby had given him, the previous night, practically everything in her larder. The place to go was the caravan. It must be well stocked. They would eat, and recover strength and spirit. Then, much later, in the dead small hours, they could mount some kind of assault on the besiegers. The thought was no more attractive, now that he was whispering among ponies over the crackling grass, than it had been in the farmhouse ten hours earlier.

Dan had only seen the caravan, briefly, two or three times. He tried to visualize it exactly. A battered Triumph 2000 had been hitched to it. Obviously it might be convenient for Eddie Birch to have a car inside the fence, as well as the various cars he had outside it. As far as Dan knew, he had not used the Triumph since the trees came down behind the caravan. Once you were on the land, the distances were very small. It was a brisk five-minute walk from the mouth of the drive all the way to the cottage at the far end of the property. They'd use the car, no doubt, if they had heavy machinery to carry. They'd use it to carry a battering ram to the front door of the farmhouse. They might even use it as a battering ram. They hadn't got to that point yet. They might never need to. Till that point, the car was likely still hitched to the caravan's towbar.

There might be men in the caravan. There might be men in the car, or men on guard round car and caravan. There was a floodlight over the mouth of the drive where the caravan was parked.

The grass crackled and rustled under Dan's knees as he crawled to the paddock nearest the road. He would have been visible there in the starlight to a man with good night vision, but for the cover given him by the ponies. He used one pony after another as a stalking-horse, to get unobserved to the bottom corner. The paddock was fenced from the drive on one side, and from the edge of the wood on the other. The fence on the south side of the paddock was the boundary of the piece Fred Mortimer had bought — the piece of which Eddie Birch was now legal tenant, filling it legally with London toughs, girdling it legally with five-strand wire.

Dan was very tired. His head ached under the bandage. He was hungry. Much of his surface was still sore from the lacerations of brambles and barbed wire. He was scared.

He examined, as well as he could in the starlight, the fence that kept the ponies from the drive. It was pretty rickety. He remembered it in general, though not in detail. He could feel the wagging of posts, the softness of rotten wood. It was a sort of post-and-rail, much patched with odd bits of timber and with lengths of rusty wire. Some of the posts were so rotten that they barely held the nails that had been driven into them, many by Dan, at all sorts of crazy angles. The old ladies hated spending money.

Dan had hatched a beautiful plan of breaking down the fence, chasing the ponies on to the drive, and stampeding them down towards the caravan. But the fence was too much for him. By day, even without tools, he thought he could have demolished part of it. He could have let all the ponies out of the paddock, even though the gate was wired up. But it was not a thing to try in the dark: especially not on a windless frosty night when the sound of a small splintering of wood would carry like a cannonshot.

He slid under the fence at the corner on to the narrow verge of the drive. He began to creep along the drive towards its mouth. Immediately there were brambles beside him. The brambles came right to the edge of the drive, which ran between high impenetrable banks of them. Once the drive had properly entered the wood, it was practically impossible to get off it. Dan thought, without enthusiasm, of the Triumph, with blazing headlights, coming down the drive towards him.

Dan saw ahead of him the glow of the floodlight over the felled trees. It should have been almost over the caravan, but it was far beyond. The caravan had been moved. It was seventy yards from the mouth of the drive, from the floodlight and the felled trees. They must have moved it in the morning when Dan was asleep, or he would have heard the noise of the car. But why had they moved it? It was an odd thing to do. It must have been more convenient for them near the road. The middle of the wood was an odd place to park it. Dan searched his mind for a reason, and found none.

There was deep shadow in front of the caravan. The car was in the shadow. Some light — not much but too much — washed up the drive as far as the car and caravan. There were patches of deep shadow cast by tree-trunks and tangles of brambles, but between them there were yards of bare, dim-lit roadway. After the corner Dan had just turned, the drive was almost straight. It had almost no verges, owing to the tide of brambles which had flowed out of the abandoned woodland. Dan went very slowly and quietly.

He heard a voice. One man at least was outside the caravan and beyond it. Presumably he was patrolling to the mouth of the drive. He was certainly wide awake. Eddie Birch had his men under tight discipline. Either he rewarded them well, or they were frightened of him. Probably both. Dan wondered where Eddie Birch was. Far away in a comfortable bed in a pub? Dan wondered if the audible sentry sometimes took a turn round the caravan. He might want to move, to keep warm, on a frosty night. He might have been told to look out for prowlers. But, as far as they knew, the only people who could come here prowling were the old ladies.

Dan wished very hard that he could have slipped off the drive into the depths of the wood. If a man came round the front of the car with a big flashlight, the wood was the place to be. But the walls of brambles hemmed in the drive as effectively as thirty strands of electrified barbed wire.

A man came round from the back of the caravan, round to the side of the car. Dan saw him silhouetted against the reflected glow of the floodlight; he could just see him beside the car, in the small amount of starlight which filtered down through the trees. Dan froze, curled like a hedgehog hard against the wall of brambles. He waited, his heart thudding, for the beam of a flashlight to rake the drive and the brambles. There was no beam. Dan heard the man open the door of the car. The car was not locked. The man was going to switch on the headlights of the car. Dan would be lit up like a fly on the lens of a lighthouse, with just as much chance of escape. He decided to jump and run, now, immediately, while there was still a split second to do so. Something held him motionless — a mixture of indecision, cramp, and something like terror. Also it occurred to him that his running feet would be heard, even if he got away quick enough not to be seen. He would be running much faster than the old ladies could run.

The man leaned into the car and asked for a light. There was another man in the car. He answered with a loud, bored swearword.

There were at least four men, awake and alert, outside the caravan, two here and two by the farmhouse. Was that the whole army? Would Eddie Birch want more men than that, to terrorize two old ladies?

The man inside the car scratched at a lighter. It flared. He held it for the man on the drive. Dan saw his face briefly. It looked uncanny, inhuman, in the brief hard light. When his cigarette was lit the man straightened beside the car. He turned slowly, inhaling, and looked up the drive. His face was turned directly towards Dan, very dimly illuminated by the glow of his cigarette. Dan tried to will himself into invisibility. He lay, rolled up into a ball so that his human profile was camouflaged, close to the brambles. He thought he must be seen. He thought he had been seen. But the man had been near the floodlight over the felled trees, and he had dazzled himself with the flare of the cigarette-lighter. He did not see Dan, or saw him only as a lump of bramble at the edge of the wall of bramble.

The man in the car ought to have seen Dan already. If he did so, or saw anything that he thought odd, he had the switch of the headlights under his hand. He too might have been dazzled by the cigarette-lighter, if he was close to it and looking at it. But not for long. It was vital for Dan to get right up to the car, almost underneath it, before the man in the car was properly on watch again, and his eyes were again used to the dark. But it was no good moving while the other man stood by the car, smoking his cigarette, quiet, alert. Dan could not move so much as an eyelash until the man went back to his post on the far side of the caravan, if that was his post. Then, when Dan did move, he might very easily find himself skewered on the beams of the headlights.

The man in the car got out of it. He got out from under the wheel, and closed the door with a bang. He too lit a cigarette, blinding himself for a little. The two men strolled to the other end of the caravan. They disappeared from Dan's view. He heard their footsteps receding towards the mouth of the drive. They were talking, in their unfamiliar London voices. One laughed loudly. They were not making any effort to be quiet. Surely they would have done so, if there had been men asleep in the caravan? Above all, if Eddie Birch was trying to sleep there. The caravan must be empty. Probably the men had slept all morning, like Dan himself, so they were awake and active now.

Dan uncoiled himself from the lip of the mountain of brambles. He prowled with a new confidence towards the car. The car itself was in the deepest darkness, in the shadow cast forward by the caravan. Dan could hear the voices from the mouth of the drive, the two men chattering and swearing. His own rubber-soled boots made no sound on the tarmac. He crept past the car, and to the near side of the caravan. His eyes, well accustomed to the not-quite-total darkness, made out two square windows. One window was broken. The caravan must be very cold. That explained, perhaps, why nobody was sleeping there. The door was on the other side. There was no suspicion of light in the windows. Dan put his ear to the thin metal shell of the caravan. There was no sound.

The side of the caravan felt sticky with frost. The tarmac of the drive was slippery with frost. The trees, arching above, barely cleared the roof of the caravan; still in full leaf, they blocked out the bright white pinpricks in the sky. Very far away a white-owl shrieked.

Dan stood as still as a mushroom, listening hard. The men by the felled trees were chattering under the floodlight. Otherwise there was no sound, no movement anywhere.

Dan went softly round the back of the caravan to the far side. He felt, with his fingertips, the off-side of the caravan. He came to the door, which was in the middle. It was open. Dan was surprised but not amazed. He was pleased. He had expected to have difficulty, opening the door without a sound.

He climbed, like a spider, into the impenetrable darkness of the caravan. In spite of the open door and the broken window and the sweet, frosty night air, there was a fug inside the caravan, a reek of socks and sausages and cheap cigarettes. Dan sniffed with distaste. He thought how much he would have hated living in such a confined space with other men, gross men who spat and scratched and spilled ash and dribbled beer, and gave off the acrid smells of the gutters of cities.

His nose twitched, exploring, like a hound's. He discerned a whiff of something completely different. It was barely perceptible over the other smells. It was clean, refreshing. It was totally unfamiliar. There was something piney about it; it was the scent of seashore pine trees under a hot sun. Dan guessed at expensive hair-oil, maybe after-shave. He had never in his life used either of these things, even in his dapper days in the bank in Milchester; he had very rarely so much as seen or smelled them. He supposed that one of Eddie Birch's gorillas fancied himself as a ladies' man or a masher; he had brought his expensive goo with him on the off-chance of a night out with the painted drabs of Milchester.

Dan hoped a broken bottle of hair-oil had not got into any of the food which he trusted was in the caravan.

Listening intently, alert as a kestrel, Dan began to grope with his fingertips amongst the jumble. He longed for his pencil flash — the only light he could have risked, if he could have risked even that. His fingers found clothes, a fallen stool, a tin kettle.

The piney scent seemed suddenly stronger than the other smells in the caravan. Dan heard a movement behind him. Crouching, he turned quickly.

Huge arms enveloped him. Both his arms were twisted behind his back, by a very strong man who knew how to do it. His arms were close to breaking. He was forced back over a knee. The piney smell hit his face, cool and refreshing and delightful.

A light blazed.

'Ah,' said Eddie Birch. 'I thought it might be you. Mallett, isn't it? I heard in the village you'd disappeared. An' I heard that nice grey pony was here. Two of my blokes had a good look at you, night before last when you were trying to get in. I thought maybe you succeeded, as they tell me you're a poacher by trade. So I put two an' two together, little man, and the sum came out perfect. Come here to nick some food, did you, for yourself an' the old witches? What you done, my son, is been an' laid a trap for yourself. I didn't have to. You done it for yourself. I think that's what they call ironic. Break his arms, Sid, so he doesn't give us no more trouble. Then we'll have a nice long talk.'

13

Eddie Birch was dressed in his smart new country-gentleman's clothes — hairy greenish suit, shiny brown shoes, shirt in little checks with short points to the collar, demure foulard-pattern silk tie. He was not dressed as a gangster, a slaughterer of ponies, a bully, a terrorizer of helpless old ladies. He was dressed as a prosperous gentleman-farmer. The health in his face, the fitness of his big body, went very well with his clothes. His thick fair hair was neatly brushed and shining; from it came a cool and refreshing scent of sun-warmed pine trees, an expensive masculine perfume which was, perhaps, a little urban and sophisticated for the rural image. Eddie Birch did not seem worried by the contradiction. He did not seem worried by anything. He sat on a stool with an electric lantern on a shelf beside him. His arms were folded. He was perfectly relaxed. He smiled at Dan.

The man holding Dan smelled different. Sweat, stale tobacco, beer; fragments of food lodged for weeks in his teeth. Dan's arms were held behind his back as though by bands of two-by-two steel. There was no give whatever in the hands he could feel; they might have been made of granite. Dan could not see the man's face. He felt and smelled his breath, which was even, relaxed, giving no indication of the slightest physical effort. The man was enormously, incalculably, stronger than Dan was. From the certainty and economy of his grip, Dan thought he was a wrestler, a combat expert with or without weapons. He probably knew some judo and karate, and a lot of dirty tricks outside those arts.

He had probably killed the pony. He smelled like a man who killed ponies.

Dan had thought he was much more frightened of Eddie Birch than of any of Eddie's men. Now he was not so sure.

Eddie Birch looked at Dan with relaxed amusement. 'Soon's they told me about that pony,' he said, 'I smelled a rat, an' you was the rat I smelled. So we moved this van up here away from the light. I thought it'd bring you. I sent a couple of blokes to hang around by the farmhouse, making sure they was where you could see them. You thought you was clever, didn't you, creeping out past them? I had the other blokes trampin' about and shoutin' to each other, so's you'd be sure to hear them. We left the van all nice and quiet, so you could get at it convenient. There's no need for my boys to be prowling round, not this time of the night. Nobody can get in, an' the old birds can't get out. But I thought, if I let you crawl round my blokes, all clever an' quiet, you'd feel lovely and confident by the time you climbed in here. That worked, eh? It's what they call psychology. That's how I succeeded in business, using psychology. Understand the criminal mentality. You are a criminal, eh? Poacher an' that? Horse-thief? An' you gone missing. Admission o' guilt, that is. I read you like a book, eh? Anticipated correctly?'

Dan nodded glumly. Everything Eddie Birch said was true. He, Dan, the prince of poachers, the slyest and subtlest night-walker in the west of England, had been hooked and played like a little trout on Dr Smith's fly-line.

'I wanted you in here quiet an' tidy,' Eddie Birch went on affably, 'like a wasp in a jam-jar. An' hey presto, here you are. Break his arms, Sid.'

There was no grunt from Sid — no intake of breath, no sign of effort. But Dan felt his arms strained in a horrible contorted position against each other and against arms and wrists like tree-trunks. The pain was frightful and it increased steadily. He expected to hear a crack and to faint from the pain.

'I'll tell!' Dan shouted.

'Cool it, Sid,' said Eddie Birch.

Through mists of pain, which made the caravan go round and Eddie Birch's calm, handsome face throb and expand like a balloon, Dan did at last hear a grunt from the ape behind him. There was no mistaking the tone. Sid was disappointed.

The pain in Dan's arms receded a little, as the appalling strain was relaxed. His arms were desperately uncomfortable, throbbing and cramped, but they were not on the edge of being broken.

'What will you tell me, Sunny Jim?' asked Eddie Birch.

Dan had no idea what he was going to tell Eddie Birch. He had nothing to tell him. He knew nothing Eddie Birch did not know, except the midnight preferences of Libby Franklin. But only talk would keep his arms from being broken. Only talk would give him time: give him, maybe, some tiny chance to get out of this mess.

'Get a move on, my son, it's late,' said Eddie Birch. 'There's a bint waiting for me in Milchester, an' I don't want her too sleepy. Squeeze a bit, Sid.'

The pain in Dan's arms increased, to a point almost past bearing.

Dan opened his mouth to talk, still having no idea what he was going to say. Some instinct made him choose his most correct banker's voice, his smooth, clipped management-trainee voice.

'If the Misses Hadfield are incapacitated,' he said, speaking clearly and slowly, as though to an important but slow-witted depositor at the bank, 'they will be unable to sign any documents relating to the sale of the property.'

'Quite true,' said Eddie Birch. 'That's why they're not dead.'

'They will be, sir, without food or water.'

'Oh no. Not yet. Stringy old things like that last better than you'd think. I saw it in the war. It's great lunks like Sid that flake out when the screws pinch. I seen that a few times too in the East End, in what they call peace-time. Those old dears will get bloody hungry and bloody thirsty, and bloody cold, and bloody sad about their ponies, but they won't peg out, not for a few days yet.'

Dan thought this was almost certainly true. The old ladies had a tremendous, defiant will to live. Eddie Birch had seen that. He knew what he was talking about. He was not going to be bluffed into fear of the imminent death of the old ladies. Dan had to try something else.

'I thought you wanted the ponies,' he said hopefully.

'I do. But I'll sacrifice one or two to get the rest. That's business sense.'

It was. Disgusting, unspeakable, but business sense.

'What would people say if they knew what you were doing to the ponies?' Dan tried.

'They won't know. If they hear, they won't believe it. I'm good news hereabouts, little man, I'm the popular local lad returned from exile to the home of his fathers. They want to believe the best of me. When I've given a bit to the Boys' Club an' a bit to the

Cricket Club an' a bit to the church roof, they'll want to believe it all the more. I'm in, laddie. If the old bits' ponies die, it's the old bits' fault. Incompetence an' lousy fencing. Nobody in the world will think different.'

It was another reply to which there was no reply. Eddie Birch had it all thought out. He was a clever man.

'There's a snag,' said Dan.

'Yeah? Try an' interest me. What snag?'

What snag? There was no snag. Eddie Birch was going to win. Ultimately he would get a signature to his papers. Then the old ladies would go into a deep hole in the ground. 'Off to Bedfordshire.' Nobody would give them another thought, and Eddie would be legal owner of Albany Farm.

The old ladies had had a joker in their hand. But now the joker was in Eddie Birch's hand. Very soon he would be torn up and dropped in the waste-paper basket. He would join the old ladies in the deep hole in the ground.

The old ladies wouldn't like sharing those cramped quarters, for all eternity, with a local odd-job man.

Dan felt weak with fatigue and hunger, and with the pain of his twisted arms, and with fright and despair. He smelled the foul, tranquil breath of Sid behind him, the fuggy reek of the over-crowded, squalid caravan, and the cool expensive hair-oil on Eddie Birch's expensively groomed head.

He said, 'I can save you time and trouble.'

'I got plenty of time. You haven't, but I have.'

'Must be an outlay, having all these men here.'

'All in a good cause. There's some of them I don't have to pay. They help me for love. Or, to put it another way, because they don't have any option. Don't you worry about my overheads. You got your own worries, boy.'

'If I may say so,' said Dan, struggling to maintain the cool authority of his best banker's manner, 'you made an error of judgement.'

'A load, I guess.'

'One in particular. That pony's leg, coming in through the window. The Misses Hadfield were on the brink of agreeing to your terms. Now they feel they cannot leave their ponies in the care of someone who . . .'

'Ah. There was always that risk.'

'They might change their minds again,' said Dan, trying to think at least as quickly as he was speaking. He was speaking slowly, but his thoughts seemed to come swimming reluctantly out of a soup of fatigue and fright. 'They might change their minds again,' he repeated, to give himself time to think what he was going to say next, 'if they could be persuaded that the pony did die as the result of an accident. If they believed that accident was the result of inadequate fencing.'

'Yeah. Who's going to persuade them?'

'I am.'

'Turn your ruddy coat? Join the other side?'

'Yes.'

'To save your own dirty little neck?'

'Yes,' agreed Dan mildly.

'By Christ,' said Eddie Birch, 'I've been offered some right instruments in my time, but I've never been offered such a treacherous little bastard as you.'

'It's like you and those ponies,' said Dan. 'Business sense.'

'They'll believe you?'

'Yes.'

'They'll sign the paper?'

'They'll need a new paper to sign. They tore the first one up.'

'Sod it. Wasteful way to behave. Downright inconsiderate. Nearest typewriter I can use is in Milchester. Let me think.'

Eddie Birch thought. He sat, silent, his face serious, visibly thinking. It was impressive. He did not try to hurry his thoughts, to jump to a decision without examining the angles. Unlike Dan, he had plenty of time. He did not care if he seemed slow, mentally ponderous, thick. He did not care what impression he made. He just wanted to make sure he was choosing the right plan.

Dan was thinking, too. With part of his brain he was willing Eddie Birch to agree to the proposition. With another part he was trying to decide what to do if Eddie refused. He measured distances with his eye. He considered movements, trying to guess what responses various movements would elicit from Eddie Birch and from Sid. He thought the distances were too great and the responses would be too quick, but a million-to-one chance was better than no chance at all.

Eddie Birch, who had been looking inwards, looked outwards at Dan. There was no particular expression in his face. He said, 'No,' with flat finality.

Dan tried to keep the despair out of his face.

'You showed you can't be trusted,' said Eddie Birch, 'so why should I trust you? You're a mischievous little bastard. I don't want you out of my sight. All the same, I can use you, use you most convenient.'

There was something now in Eddie Birch's face which sent a shiver of horror up Dan's spine, curved painfully backwards over Sid's massive knee.

'We'll carve you up slow in front of the old women,' said Eddie Birch. His manner was serious, even formal; he was like Dan's manager at the bank, long ago, announcing promotions at a staff meeting. 'We'll keep you alive, just cut off a bit at a time. We'll take as long as it takes. Simple tools — wire, wire cutters, pliers. Sid don't need anything elaborate. We've done all this before, him and me, we know how it's done. I didn't think we'd come to it this time, but I guess it's what we have come to. I think it'll work. I really think it will. I think they'll sign. If not, we'll bury the bits that's left of you, an' think of something else. But I think it's a good plan. I think it's better than your plan. 'Course, I don't expect you to agree.'

Sid laughed. A wave of his disgusting breath fanned past Dan's face from behind.

'You want Albany Farm that bad?' said Dan, hoping his voice sounded steadier to Eddie Birch than it did to himself.

'Oh yes. For my kids. Make no mistake. I do want it that bad. Now I do. Maybe I would have waited a year or two, waited till they had to give up riding school. Maybe I would have taken pity, if they hadn't lifted their bloody old noses in the air an' looked down at me like I was dirt. If they hadn't bullied my girl, my groom. If they hadn't talked like they did about my folks, about the state of the house when they come here. If they hadn't said we were pigs, when all we were was poor. But they done themselves in. My kids are going to get what they want now, straight away, no hanging about.'

With sick despair, Dan saw that Eddie Birch's plan was better than his own plan. It would work. If it didn't, nothing was lost except Dan, and a little time, and to Eddie Birch both were freely expendable.

Eddie Birch would get more documents typed up in Milchester. Eventually, half mad with horror at what was happening to Dan, the old ladies would sign them. Then they and Dan would go down into a deep hole in the woods.

Libby, snug and silent in the cottage, would never know anything about any of it. She'd accept that the old ladies had sold up, gone away. She'd wonder about Dan. She'd think hard thoughts about him for not coming back to see her. She'd remember him with mixed feelings, with a bit of resentment, with a sense of betrayal.

The dogs would feel bereft, Pansy and Nimrod and Ruby. Dan ached with longing to see them again, the assumed indifference of Pansy the cross old pointer, the liquid eyes and confiding snout of Nimrod the elegant lurcher, the scrabbling forepaws of Ruby the terrier. They'd feel bereft, and so would his mother. She'd never have the operation. She'd die lonely, in pain, in the geriatric ward of a big public hospital.

A few sleepy flies orbited round the electric lantern on the shelf by Eddie Birch's tweed-clad elbow. There'd always be flies in a pigsty, Dan thought stupidly, even in a hard first frost. The buzzing of the flies was the only sound in the caravan. The only sound outside it was the distant shriek of the white-owl.

Dan's only hope was to produce something so sudden and surprising that Sid relaxed, for a necessary split second, his crippling hold. Dan could move his head and his feet, nothing else. He also had a voice.

He used his voice. He filled his lungs and shrieked, like a white-owl, falsetto, piercingly. At the same time he lifted his left foot and shot it at the electric lantern. His heel just reached the lantern, knocking it off the shelf. It crashed to the floor. The caravan was plunged into darkness. The double surprise – two shocks, equally and utterly unexpected – distracted Sid. His arms moved, as though by the purest involuntary reflex. He did not let go of Dan, but for one startled instant his grip relaxed. It was almost enough. Dan now had to do three things at the same moment, then a number of other things immediately afterwards. He wriggled his arms clear of Sid's, and at the same time kicked backwards with all his strength into Sid's groin, and also at the same time banged his head backwards into Sid's mouth. He hurt both his head and his heel, but his head was partly protected by Libby's bandage. Sid grunted. He grabbed at Dan. But Dan was by now on the floor in the dense darkness. He picked up the smashed electric lantern and jammed it at where he thought Eddie Birch's face was. Eddie yelled and grabbed for Dan. He grabbed Sid in the darkness. Dan, skipping sideways, swept plates and pans off a shelf, to add to the bedlam in the caravan. They would expect him to try to bolt out of the door. He dived through the broken window. He felt the broken glass cutting his hands and face. He stuck half-way through, wriggled, and flopped down on to the drive. He did not fall very far. He fell partly on the tarmac and partly on the grass of the verge. The frosted ground was nearly as hard as the tarmac. The fall hurt. Dan picked himself up, half sobbing from the pain of the cuts on his hands and face, the cramped agony of his arms, and the thudding fall. He felt as though he had broken his hip. He decided he hadn't, as he was able to run. He ran away up the drive. Eddie Birch was shouting to his men. He was out of the caravan. Dan did not hear Sid. As he ran, he knew he was visible in the starlight. Nothing could be done about that. It was better to be able to run, even visibly, than imprison himself in the brambles of the woods. He heard feet pounding after him up the drive. Men were shouting. Dan thought he could run faster than Eddie Birch or any of his men.

The men watching the farmhouse, if they were still there, would hear the shouts and the running feet. They would try to intercept Dan. Dan vaulted the fence into the paddock by the drive, and made a shallow circuit round the farm. He was adding a little to his distance, but not enough to risk being caught up with. He was among ponies again. He was outdistancing the pursuit. There was nowhere to run to, in the direction he was taking, except the river.

He ran past the cottage. The cottage was between him and the pursuers, so that he was out of their sight.

There was no time to make the signal to Libby. In any case she would be in bed and fast asleep by now.

Dan paused for a second, struggling for breath, his heart pounding painfully. He had outdistanced the pursuit, but not by much. He was out of their sight, but not for long. He had planned his next move as he ran. He had very little time for it. The men, some of them, were fitter and faster than he had expected.

He ran to the rockery behind the cottage. He had helped the Morrisons make it, piling big stones and packing soil between them and planting Alpines in the cracks. He picked up a stone, a big chunk of granite. It was very heavy. When he lifted it, the rough stone hurt his lacerated hands. His head was hurting where he had bashed Sid in the mouth with it. The muscles of his arms screamed when he lifted the stone and struggled with it to the lip of the river.

He waited a second, until he was sure the nearest of the pursuers was within earshot. Then he dropped the stone into the river. It made a good loud splash. At the moment he dropped it he fell forward on to his face. He crawled very fast towards the cottage, to the corner made by the cottage wall and the back of the toolshed. He curled up into a ball in the dark corner. Almost before he was there, two men pounded across the garden of the cottage to the river bank. They were not fifteen yards from Dan. He could see them clearly in the starlight. The men could not speak for breathlessness. They were pointing at the river, at the smooth surface faintly silvered by the starlight.

One flashlight, switched on and swung round, would infallibly reveal Dan crouched in the angle of the walls. There was a flashlight. A man switched it on. He shone it at the water. The beam swung to and fro over the dark river. Two other men came up. One had one of the powerful electric lanterns. He shone it at the water. He shone it only at the water. They were all sure that Dan had splashed into the river, because, if he had known how to swim, it was the supremely obvious thing to do.

A man trotted upstream with the flashlight, another downstream with the lantern. Another light came. All the lights were directed at the water, at various points up and down the horseshoe bend of the bank.

'Swimmin' under water,' said a hoarse voice, with disgust.

'Won't last long in that,' said a shriller voice. 'It's bloody freezing.'

Eddie Birch came up, seeming as calm as though he had not just had a face full of broken glass. He disposed his men along the bank, with all available lights. He ordered them all to keep quiet, to listen to the sound of splashing. Eddie himself stayed near the cottage.

Dan uncoiled himself with infinite caution from his corner. He felt stiff and sore. His arms had not fully recovered from the contorting twists of Sid's grip. His hip felt like one huge bruise from the fall on to the road from the caravan window. His face and hands were sore and his head ached.

To make any noise would be a very bad idea. Dan went like a moth round the toolshed and the cottage to the side away from the river, the south side, where the door was, and the sitting-room window, and the window of the larger bedroom. He tapped with his fingernail on the window — short-short-long-short-short. There was no response. The bedroom window was open. Libby was asleep in bed. Dan had to tap loud enough to rouse her, but not so loud that the watchers on the river bank could hear. If she was a heavy sleeper he had problems. It seemed she was, as the shouts had not woken her.

He tapped again, louder, and again. He thought of Eddie Birch, not far away on the bank. He thought of Sid and his pliers and wire-cutters. He felt a sense of extreme urgency. He dared not throw a handful of gravel up at the window, in case Eddie Birch and his men heard. The upstairs window was only a little open — Dan could see the angle of the glass in the starlight — because of the chill of the night. Dan wondered if he could throw something in through the open window. He could wake Libby, that way, without making the kind of noise which would give him away to the pursuers. The noise would be inside the cottage. But he decided it was impossible. A stone, or his knife, would make a frightful noise on the window if he missed the narrow opening. Then he would have to run again, with nowhere to run to except the awful brambly woods. He was not sure he was capable of much more running.

He tapped again on the sitting-room window, as loud as he dared. He looked up. A mop of whitish hair appeared in the window, a pale cloud in the starlight. He waved. A moment later the door was open and Libby was in his arms.

She was appalled at the state of his face and hands. She bathed them with disinfectant in warm water. She put sticking plaster on the worst cuts. He took off his sweater, so that she could bathe the cuts on his forearms. When she had finished her ministrations he kissed her. He felt the pressure of her breasts through her nightdress and dressing-gown and his own baggy flannel shirt.

'I suppose,' said Libby into his neck, 'you'll get around to telling me how you did it. In the end. If I don't badger you.'

Dan laughed softly, although it was painful to crease his face with laughter. Keeping his voice low, he said that he had had to dive out of a window.

'A man wanted to torture me,' he explained. 'I didn't like the idea.'

'Who?'

'A bloke called Sid. I don't know his other name, if he's got one.'

'*Torture* you?'

'That's the way the conversation was going.'

'But . . .'

'Hush,' whispered Dan.

He heard footsteps outside the cottage. There was a knock on the door.

Libby called, 'Who is it?'

'Eddie Birch. I need a bit of first aid, Miss Franklin. Sorry to bother you so late.'

He still sounded quite calm. If he had lost his temper he had got it back again quick. That was another of the impressive things about him.

Libby looked at Dan, wide-eyed. Dan grimaced, and ran softly upstairs. He waited at the head of the narrow stairs in the darkness. He could see the door and part of the sitting-room into which it opened.

Libby opened the door. She gave a little scream. Eddie Birch's face was a mask of blood, far more cut about than Dan's. The broken glass of the electric lantern had minced his face into shepherd's pie.

'Not as bad as I guess it looks,' said Eddie. 'But I can't see to deal with it myself. There's a medicine cabinet upstairs in the bathroom. Ought to be some disinfectant.'

He stopped and sniffed 'I can smell disinfectant,' he said.

Dan could, too. The healthy, distinctive scent of Dettol was quite strong in the cold air of the cottage.

'You had another visitor?' said Eddie Birch. 'Another casualty?'

'No! Of course not. I put some disinfectant, um, down the lavatory.'

'Yeah? Why are you up and about this time of night?'

'Something woke me up. But what *happened*, Mr Birch?'

'Misunderstanding. I was talking to a fellow who . . .'

He stopped again. Dan craned forward, to see what had silenced him. Eddie Birch was staring at something on the sofa in the sitting-room. He could not fail to recognize it. He had been staring at it, at a range of a few feet, in the brilliant glare of the electric lantern in the caravan. It was Dan's unmistakable old sweater.

14

'So,' said Eddie Birch with terrifying gentleness. 'No visitors, eh?'

Dan could see Libby's face. She too was staring at the tell-tale sweater on the sofa. She looked like a kitten in a car's headlights.

'I've never seen that before,' she said in a high voice. 'Did you bring it in, Mr Birch?'

She was a bad liar.

'Two rats in one night,' said Eddie Birch, still gently. 'I call that a bit over the odds. I'm disappointed in you, Miss Franklin. I've treated you pretty decent. I've trusted you. Now you're giving — what's the words — giving comfort to the enemy. In fact . . .'

There was a long silence. It would have been a comfortable silence, except that it was a supremely uncomfortable one. Dan could just see the big man's face. Eddie Birch was thinking. He was looking inwards, as he had looked in the caravan before deciding to torture Dan in front of the old ladies. He was considering this new situation, and deciding what to do about it. He was taking his time. He had plenty of time. He must have guessed that Dan was still in the cottage, that he never went into the river at all. In that case Dan was trapped, with an army close at hand to find him and grab him. To grab Libby, too. Would pieces be cut off her, to make the old ladies sign the document?

'In fact,' said Eddie Birch at last, 'I reckon you changed sides.'

'What do you mean?' asked Libby, in the same high little-girl voice.

'You always was one o' their lot. Same voice, putting my teeth on edge. You looked down at me the same way they did. Pretended not to, because you was greedy, because you wanted what I was offering. Dan Mallett come an' hid in here, did he? What have you been up to, you an' him?'

All the gentleness had gone from his voice. He sounded as terrifying as he looked. The savagery of his tone went with the mask of blood on his face.

Libby opened her mouth to speak. She was very frightened. No words came out.

Eddie Birch suddenly reached out and grabbed a handful of Libby's pale untidy hair. She yelped with pain. He pulled her by her hair towards him, until her terrified face was inches from his own blood-daubed mask.

'Where is he?'

Libby was whimpering with fright, and pain, and horror at the ghastly face so close to her own. Eddie Birch was losing his temper again. He might do unspeakable things to a girl he thought had betrayed him.

Dan came down the stairs very quickly though not quite silently. Eddie Birch was too preoccupied to hear the little squeaks of the treads. Libby was sobbing loudly. It flashed into Dan's mind that Eddie had been boss so long, had terrified everybody so completely that he no longer considered the possibility of being attacked himself. He was invulnerable. He was certainly safe from assault by a funny little yokel half his size.

Dan thought Libby's choice of weapon was the best available. He picked up the big steel poker from the grate and brought it down as hard as he could on the back of Eddie Birch's head. He hit much harder than Libby had hit, because Eddie Birch had a much thicker skull than his own. The poker was not as good a weapon as his weighted blackthorn, but it was pretty good. Eddie Birch went down, almost taking Libby with him.

'You've killed him,' sobbed Libby.

'No,' said Dan, feeling Eddie's pulse. 'He'll only be out for a few seconds.'

'Oh God, when he recovers — '

'He'll start again.'

'I daren't stay here.'

'No, don't you.'

'I'll run away, on to the road.'

'You can't. It's blocked. Floodlight and guards.'

'Where can I go, then?'

'The farm.'

'Yes. Oh God. I'll get dressed.'

'No time. He's got men on the river bank. We must nip along now.'

'Oh. Yes. All right.'

She put on a tweed coat over her dressing-gown. Dan pulled on his sweater. Eddie Birch showed signs of life. Dan signalled to Libby to cover her hair, which would shine like a beacon in the starlight. She understood, and jammed an old sou'-wester over her head. It was too big for her. Dan thought she looked sweet in it, but he had other things to occupy his mind.

Easily dominant in his thoughts were those men of Eddie Birch's so very near the cottage. They were facing the other way, out over the river, because Eddie had told them to. They were sure Dan was in the river. They had lights, bright flashlights and lanterns. They'd have great difficulty seeing anything in the starlight after the glare of the lamps.

Dan considered binding and gagging Eddie Birch. Not enough was to be gained to make up for the loss of time. Eddie Birch, as soon as he was fully conscious, could make plenty of noise by banging about and kicking, unless he was tied down to a bed. That meant getting him upstairs. The prospect was daunting and far too time-consuming. The thing was to get away at once.

Dan turned off the one light, and drew Libby cautiously out of the door. He shut his eyes tight, to get them more quickly used to the darkness. He stood listening, keeping a restraining hand on Libby. Libby wanted to run away at full speed. Dan wanted the same thing, but that was not the way to do it.

'Keep your face down,' whispered Dan to Libby.

He drew her, in a crouch, obliquely across the shrubby garden of the cottage, using the shrubs as cover. They were not very good cover — forsythia, weigela, wych-hazel, viburnum — but they broke up the smooth whiteness of the starlit frosty grass. Within seconds the two were in the top paddock, among ponies, well away from the drive.

Libby suddenly whispered, startling Dan. 'Did you steal Hector?'

'Never. Hector who?'

'The grey pony. The Coxes' pony.'

'Ah. That one. Yes. Seemed best.'

They could whisper freely among the ponies, the small noise drowned by the rustling of the ponies' feet in grass crisped by the hard frost.

'What's been *happening* here?' asked Libby.

Dan thought she had seen enough of a new Eddie Birch to believe the true answer. He gave it, in a dozen words.

'Oh,' said Libby, sounding only a small part convinced. 'Why didn't the old women call the police?'

'Your boss cut the line.'

'Oh.' She digested this. 'Why didn't you call the police, from my telephone?'

'Grey pony. If the bobbies found that, they'd do sums in their funny little heads.'

'Oh. You've got an answer for everything.'

'Not everything,' whispered Dan. 'Not what to do next.'

They got into the farmhouse by the downstairs window which Dan had used, a lifetime ago, at the beginning of this uncomfortable night.

'Stand still or I shoot,' barked Miss Hettie's voice out of the darkness.

'Nay, ma'am?' said Dan, his voice broad and treacly and respectful. ' 'Tes nobbut Oi, wi' a friend.'

Dan gave a rapid and expurgated account of his adventures. As he spoke, Libby squeezed his hand, holding it tight in both hers. She was believing him. She was learning.

'I knew it,' said Miss Trixie at the end. 'You've made a complete muddle of everything again.'

'He hasn't!' said Libby, clutching Dan's hand so hard that she hurt it. 'He's wonderful. He saved my life.'

She burst into tears, but she didn't let go of Dan's hand.

'Stop snivelling,' said Miss Trixie. 'I wish I could see,' she added testily. 'Who is this person, young Mallett? How dare you bring one of your gels here uninvited?'

' 'Twere 'at,' said Dan mildly, 'or Eddie Birch a' slayed un.'

'You are presuming on your situation here to take liberties,' said Miss Hettie. 'We have been too indulgent. You are forgetting your place.'

Libby choked. She was still crying, but she was outraged. Dan put his free arm round her shoulders, and drew her face to his. He did not know exactly why she was crying.

Through her hair, he spoke across the pitch-dark room to where the old ladies were. He said, 'Eddie Birch ben a sight angry. First off, ben Oi gotten away from he. Then, a-ben Libby yere turnen out t'be on t'other side. Then, Oi bashes un on conk wi' a poker. D'set a bloke fumen, things like 'at.'

'Let him come,' said Miss Hettie. 'We're ready.'

'Nay, ma'am. Four on us, sax o' they, a-b'lieves.'

'He's got more men coming,' said Libby unexpectedly. 'From London, I think. I heard him ring up. They're coming tomorrow.'

'Gum,' said Dan. 'More sweepens o' Lunnon. Us ben short o' slape an' short o' vittles.'

'Are you suggesting,' said Miss Trixie in a voice of cold fury, 'that we give in to the detestable bully?'

'Nay, ma'am. 'Tes time t'counter-attack.'

'Of course it is. That is what I have been saying all day. However, we are two females of — of a certain age, an idiot youth, and a snivelling gel we have not even seen yet, and whose position in this whole matter is unexplained. How do you propose we counter-attack?'

Dan explained the plans which had been slowly forming in his mind. He was still talking through Libby's hair. Her body, pressed against his, was deeply pleasant but distracting. She was no longer crying, but she still wanted to hug and be hugged.

'It might work,' said Miss Hettie grudgingly, when Dan had finished. 'Well, what are you waiting for? Get on with it.'

Colonel Hadfield, as Dan knew from some of the old photographs all over the walls of the farmhouse, had been a great fisherman. His was not the temperament for little trout and delicate dry-flies; he had slaughtered huge salmon in Ireland, and mysterious monsters in the rivers of India. Faithful to their rule, his daughters had kept all his equipment in leather trunks in the attic — immense whippy greenheart rods, reels like the winches of trawlers, nets, gaffs, creels, flyboxes, hundreds of yards of powerful line.

It was the line Dan wanted.

The old ladies had given up the garden at Albany, when the gardener got too old and they were unable to cope; but it had been extensive and well equipped. Many of the tools survived, in piles in an outhouse. A bale of strawberry-netting survived.

It was the netting Dan wanted.

There was nothing that could be called a proper workshop at Albany, with bench and vice and shelves and brackets. There was simply an old wooden box with a few tools, and in it smaller boxes of nails and screws and staples. There were piles of miscellaneous wood left over from jobs, hoarded for some obscure future need.

Dan needed sharp nails sticking out of a plank, and he needed another plank with holes bored in it.

Six was too many to tackle head on. The thing was to nibble at the flanks, split the enemy up, divide and conquer. One method was something Dan had learned long ago from his father — a way of silently and secretly catching pheasants and partridges and woodcocks, rabbits and hares and roedeer. Another part of his plan was a method he had seen in cowboy films in Milchester when, almost as long ago, he had taken girls to the movies after his day at the bank.

A great deal had to be done very quickly, assembling the materials of war and making them ready for action. Most of it had to be done in the dark, since very little more light could be made in the farmhouse.

Miss Trixie, reluctantly, found Libby some clothes — jodhpurs, a shirt and sweater, a tweed coat. Her underwear was, to Libby, of a totally unfamiliar kind.

Libby said to Dan, as they worked together in the dark, 'I was crying for myself and for those children. It all seemed such a wonderful chance, so exactly what I wanted. I thought I'd be good at it. That's all gone. The moment he saw your sweater. Also, I'm very scared.'

'Me too,' said Dan.

'Have we got to be as roundabout and tricky as you said? Why not go to the cottage and ring up the police?'

'For one thing, Eddie Birch has two gorillas sitting on that telephone with guns in their hands. For another, I can't have the police here, not just yet.'

'Oh. Hector. Yes, I'd forgotten. Why exactly did you steal him, darling?'

'I thought he'd be better here. The old ladies look after their ponies very well, you know.'

'You said they couldn't be trusted at all. You said they'd put potato-peelings or something on a cut.'

'Did I? I believe I did. I wasn't quite frank with you at that stage. You wouldn't have believed the truth. You were still in love with Eddie Birch.'

'*I was not.*'

'I put that badly. You know what I mean.'

'We'd better hurry. If any of what you've been telling me is true, they're bound to attack the farmhouse. There's not very much darkness left. He's got more men coming tomorrow. I don't want to be tortured. I don't want you to be tortured. Just punished a bit, for lying to me.'

'I think we're about ready,' said Dan. 'Let's start.'

15

The first thing to do was to get out of the farmhouse, to get all of them out, while encouraging Eddie Birch to think they were all in it.

Dan lit the last two inches of candle with one of the last four matches, and left it burning in a bedroom. It was not a very subtle trick, but it ought to give the impression the house was inhabited.

He helped the others through a downstairs window, and brought all their equipment out.

The Hadfields had wanted to stay to guard their property, but Dan had convinced them — hoping he was right — that their property was safe. Eddie Birch wanted them, all four of them, and would only break into the farmhouse to get them. He did not want to damage the house or its contents any more than he had to. Also, Dan said the counter-attack depended on all four of them. Four hundred would have been better, but four was an absolute minimum.

The Hadfields thought it undignified and ridiculous to go out of the window of their own home. Dan overcame their objections. He thought that, when it came to the point, they enjoyed climbing out of the window. They had probably done it at boarding-school during the first war.

Dan took his piece of wood with nails sticking out of the end, the other piece with half-inch holes drilled in it, a pocketfull of Miss Hettie's cartridges, and several big spools of the Colonel's fishing-line. He prowled away from the farmhouse to reconnoitre.

There was nothing much to see in the starlight — the bare whitened grass of the paddocks, the ponies huddled in groups because of the cold, the shaggy bulk of the woods. There were no men anywhere near. The attack was not yet being mounted, nor an organized search attempted. Creeping further forward, Dan could see the cottage through the trees in its garden. Lights were on. Eddie Birch was still there. He must still be feeling the bang on the head. That would explain why nothing was happening yet. It wouldn't improve Eddie's temper.

There was nobody in the drive or near it. One or two of the men had almost certainly gone back to the mouth of the drive. Almost certainly some would be watching the river, not because they thought Dan had gone into it, but because they thought Dan and Libby might try to get into it. This was a cheering thought. Eddie Birch was bound to split his force.

Dan saw all there was to see, which was nothing; and heard all there was to hear, which was nothing.

He went to the edge of the wood some twenty yards from the drive, where it bordered the paddock opposite the one where the ponies were. He climbed the fence, and picked his way a few yards into the wood. He found the place he wanted, under a tree and behind a tangle of brambles. Because of the brambles, the place could only be reached from the one direction, by a passage between bramble bushes.

He put the drilled plank on the ground, exactly below the overhanging branch of a tree. He put five cartridges in the slots, caps upwards. On top of them he placed the plank with the nails sticking out of it, so that the points of the nails were resting on the nipples of the cartridges like firing-pins. The tricky part came next. Dan found, as he had been sure he would, a heavy chunk of dead wood which would have been soggy but for the hard frost. He tied each end of a short piece of fishing line to each end of the chunk. Finding the exact point of balance in the middle of this loop, he tied the end of a length of line to that point. He tossed the line over the branch above the cartridges. The starlight, here at the edge of the wood, made everything easy. He hoisted the chunk. It hung over the slat with the nails. He steadied the swing of the chunk, and made sure that it was in exactly the right place. Keeping the tension, he took the line to the fence, round a post, and a few yards along the fence. He tied it to another post. He stuck a dead branch into the fence, so that he could find the place quickly in the dark.

He crept back towards his booby-trap, careful not to trip over the line that held the chunk of wood. He laid two snares across the gap between the mounds of brambles. He chose the place exactly as he would have chosen the place for pheasant snares — across the creepway, where feet were bound to be going the only way they could. The snares themselves were like oversized pheasant snares, made of much heavier material and attached to longer lines. He tied one end of each snare to the trunk of a tree. He led the other ends back to the fence and along it, and laid them on the fence by the dead branch.

He crept back to his troops.

'What a time you've been,' said Miss Trixie crossly.

Dan made pacifying noises. He picked up the rolled strawberry-net, and led the others to the drive. It was safe to do so, for the moment. He went to the caravan, and reconnoitred it with the utmost caution. He was tempted to burgle it for food and drink, but there was no time. The battle had to be fought before dawn, and dawn was coming. With day would come Eddie Birch's London reinforcements. And then, inevitably, he or Libby or both would begin to lose fingers and other things to Sid's wire-cutters . . .

As he crouched by the caravan. Dan heard voices at the end of the drive. Two voices. Eddie Birch had put the cork back in the bottle. The important thing was that those two men were a long way from their friends.

Dan led the others a short way past the caravan, into the dense darkness of the wood, where brambles girded the drive and trees arched over it.

He uncoiled a length of the Colonel's stoutest fishing-line, to one end of which he had tied a pair of broken garden secateurs. He tossed the secateurs over the branch of a tree beside the drive. The line was now looped over the branch, at a height of twelve feet. The line ran through the mesh at the edge of the strawberry-net; Libby had threaded it before they started. On the other side of the drive, he threw the other end of the line, weighted with a spanner, over another branch. Libby held the secateur end while he pulled the spanner end. He pulled the strawberry-net clear of the ground, so that it hung right across the drive. It was completely invisible in the darkness under the trees. What Dan now had, in essence, was an old-fashioned poacher's woodcock-net. He hoped it would work in exactly the same way.

He gave Miss Trixie his end of the line, and made sure she knew exactly what to do. He made sure she had a hammer, and Miss Hettie a big wrench. Miss Hettie had her gun, too. They were both perfectly ready to use these or any other weapons, but they were very old for this sort of thing.

He stationed Miss Hettie by the net in the middle of the drive, and carefully repeated his instructions to her. He phrased them as suggestions rather than orders. She sniffed impatiently. She said she knew exactly what to do. He hoped she was right.

He disliked every bit of his own role in the operation, but it was all he could think of.

He prowled down the drive towards its mouth — towards the floodlight and the barrier of trees and Eddie Birch's two men. He kept well into the side. He kept low. He kept his face down. But there would come a moment when he must be visible. He tried to spot the two men without exposing too much of the pallor of his face to the floodlight. He saw one of them. He was sitting on the topmost of the felled trees, looking outwards over the public road. The other must be looking inwards, up the drive. By accident or design he was in deep shadow. Had he already seen Dan? Was he waiting? Was this another trap?

Dan crouched at the edge of the drive, a bare twenty yards from the barricade and the floodlight. He was uneasy. He had expected Eddie Birch's ignorant London gangsters to be pounding after him by now, lumbering blindly up the drive into the net. But they weren't being so ignorant. They were trying to lure him closer, closer, into a net of their own.

Time was rushing by. Time was on Eddie Birch's side. Every second Dan spent crouching motionless, waiting, wondering, was giving a little bit of help to the enemy.

Dan called softly into the middle of the wood, 'Summat fishy yere, ma'am. Get ye back t'paddock wi' Miss Trixie.'

As he called, he saw out of the tail of his eye that the man he could see had disappeared. Two invisible enemies. Where?

He began to trot up the drive away from the floodlight. He was horribly aware that for twenty or thirty yards he was pretty visible. He was well within range of a shotgun, let alone a rifle. He wanted to tear away up the drive, into the thick darkness. But he forced himself to run slowly, with a limp. The limp was feasible, since they knew he had dived out of the window of the caravan. The limp was not really assumed — he felt very sore and stiff — but simply exaggerated. The skin of his back crawled as he waited for a charge of buckshot in it. Eddie Birch would not want him killed, not yet, but he wouldn't at all mind him wounded.

He glanced over his shoulder. His heart jumped into his throat. The men were running and they were running fast and they were near. Earlier in the night all of them had been clumping about in heavy boots. These two had changed. They wore sneakers or plimsolls. They could move and they were moving. Dan spurted, abandoning his exaggerated limp. It was as he spurted that his rubber-soled boot met a frozen puddle. He skidded wildly. He half fell, stumbling heavily on to one knee. The two men were rushing up. Glancing back, he saw them silhouetted against the glow of the floodlight. He heard a little thin scream; he thought it was Libby, but it might easily have been himself. He somehow recovered balance and momentum and plunged forward a few feet only ahead of the pursuers.

He saw a pale blur, head high, in front of him. Miss Hettie's face. He darted past her. She was holding up the strawberry-net with the muzzle of her gun. She dropped it almost before he was through. She scuttled into the edge of the brambles. Dan ran on a few paces, then stopped and turned.

The two men, running together, ran into the net. Libby and Miss Trixie did exactly the right thing, letting go of their lines so that the net fell and engulfed the men. Dan had caught numberless woodcock in exactly the same way, in Willie Martin's river woods.

The men simultaneously tripped and sprawled when they ran into the net. Both were struggling on the ground, enveloped in strawberry-net, as helpless for a second or two as netted woodcock. Miss Hettie stepped forward and waved her gun at them. Dan took the wrench from her and waved that. Even in the dark the men could see these weapons. They were hurt from falling hard on the hard road. One was winded, gagging, unable to move. Dan tied them up very tight, ankles and wrists, with fishing-line. He taped their mouths with broad, tough, adhesive veterinary Elastoplast. The men struggled and mewed, but they were helpless.

'Two down,' said Miss Trixie grimly. 'How many more?'

'Four, mebbe,' said Dan. 'Next phase commences.'

'We've got to get them from the river bank down towards here,' said Miss Hettie. 'Shall you be a decoy again, Dan Mallett?'

'You *can't*,' said Libby, with despair in her voice. 'You were nearly caught and killed that time.'

'Clumsy boy,' said Miss Trixie. 'Can't be trusted to do the simplest thing right.'

'I think it's the moment to blow up their car,' said Dan. 'That ought to bring one or two. But we must be in the right place. It'll make a lot of light.'

'How oddly you are talking, boy,' said Miss Hettie.

'So I am,' said Dan, who had forgotten his yokel manner to the Hadfields in the heat of battle. The clotted-cream voice took too long, anyway. There was no point in reverting to it.

Dan stationed the others in places he had picked at the edge of the wood. Libby obeyed orders docilely; the Hadfield sisters accepted suggestions.

He himself went to the Triumph, still hitched to the caravan. Once again he was tempted to burgle the caravan; once again he resisted the temptation. He unrolled the long gauze bandage from the farm's medicine-chest. He opened the filler-cap of the Triumph's tank. He sniffed. There was petrol in the tank. He stuffed almost the whole of the bandage into the tank with a stick. He soaked the bandage with petrol. He pulled almost all of it out again, then led his reeking fuse away from the car. He took out the last Albany matchbox with its last three matches.

The first match broke as he tried to strike it. The head flew away, fizzing, into the frosted undergrowth. The second was damp, or had no phosphorous, or was too old. Hoping hard, Dan struck the third and last. It flared. He put it to the petrol-soaked bandage. The flame ran along the bandage towards the car. Dan flattened himself behind a tussock — he had no idea how big the explosion would be. He had never blown up a car before, and he had no idea how much petrol there was in the tank.

There was an agonizing pause. The end of the bandage had fallen out of the petrol-tank, or —

Boom.

The vapour in the tank, the petrol itself, exploded. There was a brilliant white-orange flare, another boom. The car was burning merrily.

The fire vividly lit up the drive and the fencing of the paddocks, the tangle of brambles and the over-arching trees. The flames seemed certain to scorch the nearest trees, but Dan thought a forest fire unlikely in the windless frosty air. He ran away from the glare of the fire, along the edge of the wood where he had planted his next trick. He was in deep shadow again, as the corner of the wood hid the burning car. Once over the fence and into the edge of the wood, he would be in almost total darkness.

As he was sure would happen, men ran down towards the burning car from the direction of the cottage. He saw two men. Neither one was Eddie Birch; neither one was Sid. There might be another man behind the two, nervous of an explosion, or a slower mover, or tired, or under different orders from Eddie Birch. Dan waited until the two men he could see were near the car. They stood by the edge of the wood. They realized, obviously, that there was nothing they could do. They were held, as anybody would be, by the fascination of the fire. Maybe one of them was the owner of the car. They were well within earshot of a bang, in spite of the hissing and coughing of the burning car.

Dan groped along the fence until he found the branch he had stuck into it. The branch led him to the line which he had tied to an upright. He untied the line and held it. It tried to pull out of his fingers.

The two men might be joined by others, by Eddie Birch and Sid. That would be disaster. The two of them could be dealt with, but not more than two.

Dan let go of the line. The weight of the chunk of timber whisked it out of his fingers. The chunk thudded down on to the slat, and drove the nails into the percussion caps of the cartridges. All five cartridges exploded simultaneously. The bang was considerable; Dan, expecting it, jumped. It was the second bait in his trap, drawing the men towards the place he had chosen for them. It was working. He saw two startled faces turn towards him from the drive, pale in the glare of the flames.

The men seemed to confer for a moment. One of them ran back up the drive towards the farm. Dan thought for a moment he had gone to report, or to get reinforcements. But he saw him climb the fence into the paddock, and make a big circuit towards the bang they had heard. They were being sensible, approaching the shooter from two sides and so cutting off his escape. They would go carefully when they got within shotgun range. They knew about Miss Hettie's gun. The other man climbed into the paddock at the corner and came slowly along the edge of the wood, directly towards Dan. He would not be seeing well in the dark after the glare of the fire.

Dan slipped over the fence into the edge of the wood. He held his two other pieces of line. He waited, watching and listening.

The man who was coming straight from the car had flattened himself. Dan could no longer see him, but he knew he must be crawling forwards. Before he rushed the shooter he would wait for his friend to come up.

The other man had made his circuit and was coming along the fence from the other direction. He passed Dan, crouching, moving as softly as he could. Dan saw him clearly against the frosty starlit grass of the paddock.

Probably they had lights. But they would not use them to make targets of themselves for the shotgun. They would expect the shooter to have reloaded, to have cartridges in both barrels. They knew pretty well where the bang had come from. Their eyes by now used to the darkness, they would rush the shooter, both together hurling themselves down the narrow alley between the brambles. A sudden rush was by far the best and safest plan for them.

Now the two were reunited. They had made sure the shooter had not got away across the paddock. They knew he could not get away quietly through the brambles of the woods. They knew where he was. They had him cold. They charged him. They probably thought they were charging Miss Hettie.

As they rushed down the passageway between the brambles, Dan felt a violent jerk on one of his lines, then immediately on the other. He pulled the lines as hard as he could. There were bumps and crashes as the men upended into the brambles and into the passage between the brambles. Dan hauled with all his strength on the two lines; he felt as though he were handling two enormous fish.

Holding his lines, shortening them as he went, Dan hurried to the passage between the brambles. He could just see a writhing mass of limbs, half in the brambles. He hauled on one line. There was a screech, as the noose bit hard into a leg. He pulled the leg out of the scrummage. It was fast in the invisible snare. With a certain feeling of guilt, Dan took a monkey-wrench out of his hip pocket and hit the man hard on the head before he had a chance to get up. The other snared man was struggling to his feet. Dan yanked the snare that held him. The man staggered and fell on one knee. Someone stepped up behind him and hit him on the head. He grunted, but did not fall. Miss Hettie came up, and prodded him in the chest with the muzzle of her gun. The man whimpered and surrendered, unable to cope with hazards he did not know and could not see.

Dan tied the two men up with fishing-line, and taped their mouths with veterinary Elastoplast.

'How many more of the wretches are there?' asked Miss Trixie. 'You are using up all our sticky tape. It is very expensive, you know. And I am tired.'

'Rubbish, Trixie,' said Miss Hettie. 'This is no time for whining.'

'I am not whining, Hettie. I merely remarked —'

'Two, I think,' said Dan. 'Eddie Birch and my friend Sid.'

'Daylight coming,' said Libby.

After a period of tremendous energy, Dan felt bottomlessly tired. He felt incapable of thought. He tried to think.

He thought: Eddie Birch must know pretty well, by now, what was going on, and how it was being done, and why, and who was doing it. Men were going out and not coming back. But he still had Sid. He and Sid were enough to deal with two old ladies, a runt of a poacher, and a frightened young girl. They simply had to be careful, and to wait until daylight. Two big men hardened in the school of East End in-fighting were plenty for what Eddie Birch had to do. He would sit tight, and mop up at leisure by daylight. And if he found any problems, he had an army coming sometime during the day.

They approached the cottage without seeing anyone. Dan parked the others behind a hazel clump. He crept to the wall of the cottage. Lights blazed in every room; a warm glow came out through the curtains. The cottage was silent. Dan could not believe Eddie and Sid were asleep, even though they were not planning to do anything until daylight.

There was no sound at all from the cottage: no hint of the smallest movement.

Dan realized suddenly that Eddie Birch was doing exactly what he would have done himself — what he had done, hours before. He had left an empty house with lights burning to suggest that it was not empty. He had moved himself and Sid to — where? Was an ambush lurking in the garden? Somewhere on the farm? No, not in the frost, not coddled Londoners. They were in the farmhouse. They must be. Eddie had shifted his headquarters, taken possession of the citadel.

Leaving the telephone unguarded? Obviously not. Wire cut: must be.

The cottage was probably booby-trapped — spring gun, bomb, mantrap, electricity — Sid was probably good at games like that.

Or the lights and silence might be double-bluff. They might be not in the farmhouse but here, hiding, waiting to jump.

All they needed was one prisoner. They'd probably choose Libby, if the choice offered. Then Sid got busy with his wire-cutters, and all resistance ended. Or daylight came, and the reinforcements, and all resistance ended.

Dan wondered if he could open the door of the cottage by remote control — perhaps with a long stick — and drive a pony in. But he did not want to subject a pony to Sid's booby-trap. And if it was an ambush rather than a booby-trap, nothing would happen. Nothing would be proved.

Dan wondered how to find out if there was anyone in the cottage without taking a suicidal risk. He was still wondering when he rejoined the others behind the hazel.

'They may be there,' said Dan softly. 'They may be in the farmhouse.'

'What?' said Miss Trixie, outraged.

'But I don't know which, and I don't know how to find out. If I go in through the door or look in through a window, I'll have my head blown off, maybe. That might happen here, or it might happen at the farmhouse.'

'They can't stay there for ever,' said Miss Hettie, 'either here or in our house.'

'They won't have to,' said Dan, 'with Eddie's other friends arriving in a few hours.'

'Bringing their own tools,' said Libby, remembering. 'Does that mean guns?'

'Yes,' said Dan. 'We must finish this tonight. We must finish it in the dark.'

'We could burn the cottage down,' said Miss Hettie. 'And I'll shoot them as they come out. Just in the legs, you know.'

'They'll come out the other side,' said Dan, 'through a window, wherever you aren't.'

'In any case, you finished up all our matches, you silly boy,' said Miss Trixie.

They pondered, squatting in silence behind the hazel clump. Dan could see no way of finding out which building Eddie Birch and Sid were in, without being killed. Even if he knew which house they were in, he could see no way of getting at them without being killed.

Terribly soon it would be daylight. Reinforcements were coming from London.

The woodcock net had been fine, for the two suckers it had caught. The bangs and snares had been fine, for the two they had caught. Nothing like that would catch Eddie Birch and Sid. In the end, all Dan had achieved was to put Eddie Birch into a murderous rage. He was going to kill all four of them in the next eight hours or so. And one of the four would be killed slowly — himself or Libby — so that the old ladies would sign the paper that said they were selling Albany. After that, the old ladies themselves might die quite quickly. They would certainly, infallibly, inevitably die.

Dan could see absolutely no end to the situation.

'What are we to do?' asked Miss Hettie after a long pause. In her voice, for the very first time, there was a tremor of frightened misery.

Dan looked helplessly round at the frosty garden. He could see the shrubs a very little more clearly. He could see the white post-and-rail fence at the top of the paddock. The first beginnings of dawn were spilling up a milky pallor from the east in the sky over Milchester. Dan had to do something. He had no idea what to do. Every second the light was strengthening. He saw the white, exhausted faces of the old ladies, and the white hair straggling down from their bowler hats. He saw Libby's white face, tired and frightened.

He saw, a dozen yards away, a familiar white shape, rectangular, a yard high: the old ladies' beehive, kept in the cottage grounds so that the ponies couldn't knock it over.

Into the exhausted muddle of his mind came, idiotically, Libby's words when they first made love in her bed. She'd said he was like a honeybee, small and brown and busy and buzzing, looking harmless but carrying a sting . . .

'Bees,' said Dan.

The old ladies glanced at each other, as though silly chatter was all they might have expected from Dan.

'We'll pop a few frames into a bag, and push them into the cottage through a window.'

'The bees will be *very* cross,' said Miss Trixie.

'Yes, ma'am. I think they'll tell us if there's anybody in there.'

'We did not bring veils or gloves out with us,' objected Miss Hettie.

'We do not need them at night,' said Miss Trixie. 'A sting or two will not hurt you.'

They had nothing which would do as a bag, except a garment from any one of them. Dan found himself chosen as the provider of the garment. The Colonel's flannel shirt was better than his sweater, which was loose-knit and extensively torn. He stripped to the waist, shivering, and pulled the sweater on quickly over his bare shoulders. Miss Trixie tied up the arms of the shirt, buttoned the buttons, and sealed the neck and part of the skirt with the last of the veterinary Elastoplast. The result looked ludicrous, but it would hold a few bees for a few minutes.

Dan went to the hive, the old ladies following. He was extremely aware that their tweed coats and bowler hats and breeches gave them much better protection than he had. But he knew he had to do the next bit. Libby kept well away. She had no experience of bees. Dan thought she was wise.

Dan took off the square top of the beehive. There was a crunch of frosted grass as he laid it on the ground. He looked down into the hive. Although dawn was rushing up the sky, he could see nothing. He groped down, visualizing what his hands would meet. He felt the oblong frames of honeycomb resting on their slats, crawling with sleepy bees. He knew that handling bees without gloves and veil was a matter of speed and certainty; you had to do as much as you could before the bees woke up and lost their tempers. He worked fast. He lifted out the first light wooden frame, packed solid with honeycomb. The honey had already been spun out of the cells by the separator. The cells were full of bees. Bees clung or crawled all over the wax and the wood. Miss Trixie held out the bag which was Dan's shirt. Dan put the fame gently into it. He was stung twice. Miss Trixie said, 'Drat . . . Drat.' Apart from that she was stoical about being stung. Miss Hettie was more stoical still. She said nothing, although she must have been stung too.

The bees were waking up. Dan quickly put eight more frames into the shirt, and Miss Trixie bundled up the tail of the shirt to keep the bees in. Some of the bees would sting the flannel, killing themselves, but nothing could be done about that.

They retreated, rapidly, well away from the beehive. The sleepy hum had risen to a furious roar. Dan took the shirt from Miss Trixie. He was immediately stung three times by escaping bees.

He prowled round to the other side of the cottage, using the cover of the shrubs, and to the cold-frame which the grey pony had destroyed. He found a loose half-brick amongst the broken glass and shattered timber. He slid round the corner of the cottage, keeping flat to the wall. More bees escaped from the shirt. He lost count of the number of times he was stung. Plastered to the wall, he edged to the sitting-room window.

If anyone looked out of an upstairs window, opened it and looked down, Dan must be seen. A lovely target, stationary, clearly visible in the pearly dawn light.

Dan broke the window with the half-brick. The window gaped on to the drawn curtain behind. Almost before the glass had stopped tinkling, he emptied the bees out of his shirt into the room. He heard the light wooden frames clatter innocuously on to the floor of the sitting-room. He heard the bees explode into the room, very angry indeed. Dan fled to the shelter of a big escallonia bush.

The whole of this might be a complete waste of precious time. The cottage might be empty, and the bees deprived of victims.

They were not deprived. There were bellows of agony and terror from the cottage. It occurred to Dan that Eddie Birch had probably had no contact with a bee since he left Albany at the age of five; and Sid, a creature of concrete, had probably never seen a bee at close quarters in his life. Half a swarm, in a fury, in the confined space of a small room, would seem like a visitation from hell.

The cottage door burst open. An enormous man came out like a boar-pig released from a box, tearing out, thundering, screaming. Dan saw that it was Sid. A cloud of bees came with him, their buzzing having the high pitch of fury. Sid ran round the cottage, still screaming. He tripped and fell heavily. He picked himself up and staggered towards the river. He threw himself into the water. He would have thrown himself into boiling oil or quicklime or acid to get away from the bees.

Dan trotted to the river bank, interested to see if Sid's manœuvre worked. Miss Hettie joined him, her gun under her arm.

Sid was trying to swim under water. He was heavily dressed for the frosty night, and his clothes hampered him. There was still plenty of thick, trailing weed in the river, not yet knocked back by colder weather. Sid made poor progress. The bees swirled over him, a tight black cloud inches from the water. Sid surfaced and looked about him. Bees snarled at his face. He yelled and submerged himself. The bees stayed with him.

'Silly fellow,' said Miss Hettie. 'He's doing quite the wrong thing.'

'If he stays in that water long,' said Dan, 'he'll catch a nasty cold.'

'If he comes out he'll catch a bee or two.'

'One or two,' agreed Dan. 'I wonder which he'll choose.'

Sid chose the water. He was wallowing like a whale. Long tendrils of vivid green weed had wrapped themselves round his legs and his shoulders. The dawn had turned the surface of the river into steel: it swept unbroken round the horseshoe bend. Sid had got himself far out into the river. He was being swept downstream. He carried with him a huge, clogging island of trailing weed. His shouts were becoming thinner and his splashing feebler. He was faithfully attended by his black cloud of furious bees. Within two minutes he was almost out of sight round the bend in the river. Hampered by his heavy clothes and by the great rafts of weed, he seemed unable to swim to either bank. Maybe he was still unwilling to expose himself to the bees, even though the ice-cold water must be chilling him to the bone.

'I don't see any way of helping him,' said Dan.

'We couldn't save him,' said Miss Hettie. 'And we wouldn't if we could.'

'He'll be dead by the time he gets to the village. Drowned or frozen.'

'Nobody will see him at this hour. He'll drift straight through the village and out the other end. I suppose he'll get caught up in a hatch somewhere. Will they call it accident or suicide? It must be one or the other. *We* never touched him. Never laid a finger on him. Poor man. What a horrid end.'

Sid disappeared round the bend in the river. He was hardly moving. The wide smooth surface of the river was turning from steel to milk as the sky paled over Albany. The sky was clear, a hard bright grey with the beginning of a wash of yellow to the east. It was very cold. There was still a hard frost. A song thrush began to pipe very softly from the middle of a leafless lilac. The song was thin, reedy, uncertain, as though the bird had forgotten how to sing, as though it knew a frosty dawn was a silly time to be singing.

Dan shivered in his inadequate sweater.

There was no sound from the cottage, except the quieter buzz of a great many bees. Their fury was leaving them. They were sleepy. The lights in the cottage still blazed, shamed by the strengthening daylight.

Miss Trixie stumped across the grass to join her sister on the river bank. Libby followed. Miss Trixie looked infinitely old and exhausted, but she held her back straight and marched across the rough grass in full view of the cottage.

'There can't be anybody else in there,' she said. 'The man Birch must be hiding somewhere else.'

'Seems so,' agreed Dan. 'But it's odd. I thought they'd stick together, those two.'

'I'm glad we didn't burn the cottage down, if he's not there,' said

Miss Hettie. 'It would have been a waste just for one of them. Although I still think it was a good idea.'

'Nonsense, Hettie. We had no matches. In any case, we shall be needing it. That is to say, if you are thinking of going on living there, dear.'

After a puzzled pause, Libby said in a small voice, 'Do you mean me?'

'Yes, of course. My sister and I have decided to retire from active management of the riding school. Will you consider joining us? We can pay you an excellent salary, since we have Mr Birch's cheque for £100,000.'

'You can't keep that money!' said Dan.

'Oh yes we can,' said Miss Hettie.

'You are a girl of resource and courage,' said Miss Trixie to Libby. 'I forget your name at this moment, but I expect I shall get used to remembering it. My father would have approved of you.'

'Oh,' said Libby. She burst into tears.

'Not of those waterworks,' said Miss Hettie. 'He wouldn't have approved of them at all.'

Dan said carefully, 'About that money, ma'am. There's the kids to consider. Eddie Birch did all this for them. It's their money, seems to me.'

'I know he did it for them,' said Miss Trixie. 'And of course he was quite right.'

Dan looked at her in astonishment. Libby's mouth had dropped open too in surprise.

'It was natural,' Miss Trixie went on calmly, 'that he should want them to have Albany. They shall have it. Not at once, but in the fullness of time.'

'Oh,' said Dan, stunned. 'That's good.'

'Of course,' said Miss Hettie, 'they should be removed from the pernicious influence of that dreadful father. They will be better here, in the school holidays.'

'Their father may not agree,' said Libby unexpectedly.

'He will be in no position to agree or disagree,' said Miss Trixie, 'when we have finished with him. Where *is* the man? In our house? Or do you suppose he's run away?'

'When Sid came galloping out,' said Dan, 'I was certain Eddie Birch was still inside. I couldn't believe those two would go off separately. Sid was Eddie Birch's chief of staff, right-hand man, executioner. He told me himself they'd been in all kinds of capers in London together, cutting off fingers and such . . . He *must* be in there.'

'I think I heard two lots of yelling when the bees went in,' said Libby.

'A good point, dear,' said Miss Trixie. 'It confirms my own impression. Two men *did* shout. I'm sure of it.'

'Well then,' said Miss Hettie, 'he can just stay in the cottage with the bees until he gets too hungry to stay there a moment longer.'

'No, ma'am,' said Dan. 'His reinforcements are coming today. We don't know what time. We must deal with Eddie Birch before they get here. Maybe we could . . . no.'

'You're cold,' said Libby.

'Yes. I'll put that shirt on.'

Dan went cautiously to the broken window. The shirt lay on the ground below it. He put his ear to the jagged gap in the glass. He could hear bees, but nothing else at all.

How could a man stay silent and motionless in the midst of those bees? It was impossible. Was he, could anybody be, so stoical, so determined, so tough, that he sat quiet in ambush all alone, deserted by his lieutenant, with bees stinging every bit of him that showed? It was impossible. Nobody had that degree of self-control. Eddie Birch must be somewhere else. Dan became certain of it. The two different yells that Libby and Miss Trixie had heard must have been Sid yelling in two different keys.

Dan pulled off his old sweater, and resumed the Colonel's flannel shirt. A couple of sleepy bees, lurking in the folds, stung him in the small of the back.

'Drat,' he said, since Miss Trixie had made it the night's acceptable word for complaining of bee-stings.

If Eddie Birch was in the cottage, he must have been stung a hundred times, two hundred. If 'drat' was forced out of Dan and Miss Trixie, something would have been forced out of him, something beyond an initial astonished yell. At the very least he would have rushed upstairs, banged doors, made some sort of commotion.

Dan could not have failed to hear him. There had been no noise of that kind — no noise of any kind — after Sid's frenzied eruption. Therefore the cottage was empty except for bees.

Dan convinced himself of this. He glanced up at the brightening sky. He wondered what time Eddie Birch's reinforcements were due. He was tired, but not as tired as the old ladies. He needed food, but not as badly as they did.

It had to be done sometime. It had to be done now. Dan went to the cottage door and opened it boldly. He heard a little cry from Libby. He heard the hum of sleepy bees. The electric light blazed in the sitting-room. There were bees everywhere, in drowsy clumps on walls and furniture. A chair had been upset and a small table smashed.

Dan looked round anxiously. The kitchen door was open. Dan went gingerly towards it, avoiding bees on the floor. The lights blazed in the kitchen, too. There were more bees there.

Eddie Birch lay on the kitchen floor. He was surrounded by dead bees. Dozens of the little brown furry corpses clung to his face and hands and wrists and exposed ankles. There were others all over his clothes, and on the linoleum round him. His eyes and mouth were wide open, frozen in a mute scream.

Maybe a heart attack. Maybe the venom of so many beestings. Maybe he was allergic. Maybe terror helped. Anyway the bees had done it. Nothing else. No person. It was death by misadventure.

It was ironic, thought Dan. Such a powerful, confident juggernaut of a man, done in by a handful of honeybees.

He collected the frames of honeycomb from the floor in front of the broken window. They must go back into the hive. Then it was misadventure indeed.

He went out of the cottage. It was full daylight. Libby was sitting on the grass, looking near collapse. The old ladies were still indomitably standing.

'Been a terrible accident,' said Dan.

'Oh dear, I am sorry,' said Miss Trixie, in a tone of conventional regret.

'Then it is time to get the police here,' said Miss Hettie. "May we use your telephone, Elizabeth?'

'Yes,' said Libby in a muffled voice.

'Just a minute,' said Miss Trixie. 'There are one or two things to be considered.'

'Matter of a grey pony,' said Dan apologetically.

'I suppose,' said Miss Hettie, 'you will insist on removing the one I bought at Milchester market.'

'If I may,' said Dan, who had been wondering how to smuggle the animal away.

'You admit at last — ' said Miss Trixie triumphantly to her sister.

'I admit nothing. The other pony still has an injured leg. It must stay here. That being so, my pony will have to go. I regret it extremely. That animal would have been very useful to us, and we were lucky to get it so cheaply. I will say no more than that.'

'I'll cut a gap in the wire,' said Dan, starting to move off before Miss Hettie could change her mind.

'I'll come and help you,' said Libby.

They went back to the mouth of the drive, checking up on their four prisoners on the way. Dan climbed the barricade of trees and went out on to the road. There was no sign of a car. He walked the full distance of the perimeter. At the western end, where the road met the river, he found the two searchlight cars parked on the verge. There was nobody in or near them. They were both locked.

Dan found tools in the caravan, as he expected. There was plenty of tinned food there, too. The old ladies took all they could carry, while Libby caught the grey pony from Milchester. Dan disconnected the alarm and snipped the barbed-wire with big wire cutters from the caravan.

He kissed Libby and rode the pony away, bareback, towards the village. There was nobody about in the freezing dawn. All the fields and hedges were starched with hoar frost. Dan's hands, without gloves, got so cold he could hardly hold the reins. He rode not into the village but towards home, to the cottage under the edge of the Priory woods. He dismounted a hundred yards short, unbridled the pony, and gave him a friendly slap on the rump. The pony began to graze the frosty grass of the verge.

Dan found his mother in bed, but wide awake and worried.

'Everything's fine,' he told her. 'Problems all solved tidy.'

'Ye ben wi' a wench all this time, then?'

'Not all of it. I'll have to go back to Albany, old lady. Can you manage with your breakfast one more time? I'll be home when I can.'

'What do I tell they policemen, so be they comes again?'

'Tell what happened,' said Dan. 'I came home an' I went off. But I don't think they'll bother you today.'

She grumbled at his leaving, but only because she was still worried for him. He reassured her as best he could, but it was necessary to get back to the battlefield. The sooner the police were called the better, now that they could be called.

He changed out of the Colonel's ridiculous clothes into clothes of his own, and found some sheepskin mittens. He bicycled as quickly as he could back to Albany, getting warm for the first time in many hours.

The old ladies and Libby were having breakfast in the drawing-room of the farmhouse, where they had made an enormous fire. They were warm, and so was the breakfast.

'I'll go and telephone,' said Miss Trixie, finishing her third cup of coffee. 'But I want to be clear about one thing. The night you moved the pony here, Dan Mallett, which of course you did *not* do — '

'Yes, ma'am?' said Dan, his mouth full of hot tinned spaghetti.

'It was the night immediately after the gymkhana, was it not? Of course you were working here late, helping us to clear up. So that we suggested you stay here the night. You were in the farmhouse all night. You could not have moved the pony or anything else. We can vouch for that, Hettie, can we not?'

'The idle boy was too lazy to bicycle home,' said Miss Hettie. 'Also he had no lamp for his bicycle. We allowed him to stay. I remember distinctly because it was thoroughly inconvenient.'

Dan nodded his thanks. His mouth was too full for speech.

Miss Trixie went off to dial 999. She reported the siege, the threats, the killing of the pony, the accidental death of Eddie Birch, the prisoners they had taken, and the damage to some of the honeycomb-frames of her beehive. She said the men were all gangsters from London, of whom more were said to be arriving shortly.

'The man didn't believe a single word I said,' she said angrily as she hung up.

Nevertheless a lot of policemen came remarkably quickly, with two cars and a Black Maria and a doctor and a photographer. The Detective Sergeant with the face like a Hereford bull took long statements from the Hadfields, Libby and Dan. The telephone was in constant use. Several of the policemen were stung by sleepy bees in the cottage.

The men Dan had tied up were untied and arrested. They all needed first aid. They were very cold.

The Sergeant, after taking his twentieth telephone call, said that a body had been pulled out of the river four miles below Medwell. It was identified as Sidney Millikin by a driving license which had kept dry in a plastic holder.

The police carried out a thorough search of the farm, the cottage, and the woodland which Eddie Birch had rented. They found Hector in his loose-box, and a young detective thought he looked like the pony which had been reported stolen. Miss Hettie showed them the receipt from the Milchester auctioneers, which confirmed her recent purchase of a 13-hand grey pony. There was no other pony answering this description at Albany. Libby said the pony was not the one of which she had had charge.

The Sergeant still thought Dan had something to do with the missing pony and the missing clocks. But there was nothing he could do about it.

Long messages came on the telephone from London. Eddie 'Silver' Birch had no criminal record since his 'teens, when he had spent a year in Borstal. He was known as an associate of criminals. Some of his business rivals had disappeared but nothing had ever been pinned on him. Underworld rumours about his wife were unconfirmed; she was in a mental home in Essex. Sid Millikin was identified as a hard, violent South London tough who had spent twelve of his thirty-eight years in prison; he was currently suspected of running a small-time protection racket in betting shops and discos.

Two car-loads of secret-faced men arrived at midday. They said they had been sent for by a Mr Edward Birch, who had labouring work for them. None of them admitted to having met Mr Birch. None had the clothes or boots or hands of labourers. Guns and other concealed weapons were found on them. They were accordingly arrested.

Telephone, electricity and water were restored to the farmhouse during the afternoon.

A timber merchant in Ighampton sent a gang, with a lorry, to clear the felled trees. They turned the trees into firewood with power saws and axes; they stacked part of it in the Albany woodshed as payment for the rest.

A man came out from Milchester to repair the windows of the farm and the cottage.

The vet came and looked at Hector's shin. He changed the dressing, and complimented Miss Hettie on her care of the pony. He said there would be a scar but no other permanent damage. He was surprised to hear that the Hadfields had found such a high-class animal in Milchester market.

A garage removed the caravan and the burned-out shell of the Triumph.

Bert Monger sent his van from the village shop with a big order of provisions for the Hadfields and for Libby.

Libby asked Dan to supper at the cottage. He accepted.

Dan told the police he would be available to give evidence at the inquest on the death of Edward Birch, the inquest on the death of Sidney Millikin, and the trials of the others. He was allowed to go home to feed his pigeons, his bantams, his dogs and his mother.

When he got home soon after six, he had to insert his bicycle into the shed knee-deep in hungry bantams. Gloria, most confiding of his hens, fluttered on to his shoulder and whispered in his ear. She pretended it was love but it was greed. He fed the dogs and gave them a run, and then made a sort of Irish stew for his mother. He ate a little of it to keep her company, but he did not want more than one and a half dinners.

The white-owl was shrieking when he bicycled between the Albany paddocks.

Libby's face was pink when he kissed her. She was trembling.

An hour after he arrived they had supper on the hearthrug in front of the sitting-room fire. Libby was wearing her old blue dressing-gown, Dan a blanket from her bed. When she put down her empty coffee-cup, Dan leaned forward and undid the sash of her dressing-gown. It fell open. She smiled and blushed. At that moment Dan was stung in the buttock by a sleepy bee which was hiding in the folds of the blanket. He hardly felt it.